VOWS

A Novel

VOWS

A Novel

By

Anna Lee Walters

soje

PUBLISHING

Vows

Anna Lee Walters, editor
David Moratto, interior design
Soje Publishing

First edition.

Library of Congress Control Number: 2014918471

Dedication

I dedicate this work to the memory of the late Truman Dailey and to so many others like him. Of course through time there have been hundreds, far too numerous to mention individually, but all are remembered for their vision and ways of life.

Acknowledgments

The music appearing at the beginning of each part in this manuscript was recorded by Frances Densmore and is preserved in her book, *Cheyenne and Arapaho Music.* It was first published by the Southwest Museum (Southwest Museum Papers, Number 10) in 1936. That she had the foresight to study and record this part of Native American life is fortuitous for later generations.

Contents

xiii

PART ONE
New Fire

Opening song

RECORDED BY KISH HAWKINS

Lily

ᴇᴀʀʟʏ sᴛʀᴇᴀᴍs ᴏғ light strike the house and she appears outside. She's wearing bulky work clothes, watching others in the distance lift long slender poles upright until it's all done. The tipi stands up and a solitary eagle feather flutters gently above. Much later, in sun's afterglow, she enters the empty white pristine tipi to sit in a solitary pose on clean, swept ground, her long soft white floral skirt tucked loosely around her bent legs. New fire strums at the center of the tipi, throwing out welcome and solace all around.

Serenity...

Taut muscles soften, melt in her face and body, slowing her breath until it becomes an imperceptible thread, and then a low sigh breaks the evening quiet. Her eyes follow the smooth poles skyward, looped together securely at the smoke hole; next her gaze traces a gentle curve of the earthen altar rising off ground and moves on toward bursting, popping, twirling flame. Then words, at rest in her mind, stir and revive like very ancient teachers unvisited for a while.

Breath... Words... Story...

Red flames whoosh, crack! Murmurs of long departed storytellers open her up to an unbroken rhythm of life unleashed way before she came along. Facing the fire, all the yesterdays it keeps swoosh toward her, alive, beckoning. Then gliding images of people traveling in loose lines appear, first on foot and next atop exuberant spirit horses. The images faintly take off, coming fully to life before her. Flesh and blood. Warm. Breathing.

They are spirals of wind stroking sleeping land, parting and bending tall yellow grass on wide, descending plains. Robust men and women eagerly step forward in vaporous dawn to follow and make trails into it, tamping the ground, leaving intended and unintended impressions while older bent figures cross more slowly in waves behind the first with leaping and racing children, the friction of all their moving bodies leaving faint florescent streaks in space, like traces of shooting ash at the center of the tipi.

Their devotion to each other and to their journey together spark in warm agate eyes, and under high new flame, in falling, pulsating, orange embers turned white and gray when they sprinkle the ground, is the touch and go of daily life.

Halting, those people glance behind them at disappearing trails they have finished to count their losses, and ahead at ones glimmering in wait. They gaze across intense hot, white, whirling suns and melting snows at Lily. Then they move on.

What's gone before... Always here...

Popping flame, at first a faint single sound, becomes a hum, a chorus of their voices, lilting. Red embers fling, coinciding with their tireless gestures, as Lily sees them reach out to clutch one another, bring each other to safety right then and there, and into the next sun and next season.

Words... Story... Acts....

Breaking their lines and parting when they're too many, pockets turn with arcs of shiny flowing water and animals running and panting, and stay in close proximity to each other. By then, their frugal camps and towns pop up on changing horizons as rapidly as they go down, while bands of distinctive men and women vow to remain united, chasing game, visions, and destroyers venturing near.

"Family and relatives we are," they declare, "as long as there is wind!"

Alien people... Distant land... Unknown ground...

Spontaneous images keep forming, with rushing sounds and fragments of breathy speech. Pictures of them decisively taking human life, and, at other times, sparing it, or giving birth. Spilled blood.

Frightful in war, ferocity is their banner. With deadly cunning and aim, they strike as one smooth, heavy, whizzing and hurling stone ax—always one strike, one heartfelt thump. Spilling blood, sharp fierce cries of "Aaiiee!" stab peaceful valleys and ridges, echoing afar, briefly silencing, stunning, animals and birds quietly poised there, pinning startled creatures where they are—before madly scattering in squalls across the horizon and higher up in a great flapping of wings and whipping of air! "Aaiee!"

They watch enemies drop in thuds, lifeless, mute. Looking coolly toward Lily, they set their jaws, turn and move on.

Then joy arises in their camps over life given or prolonged; their voices and chants billow in all directions. Peace prevailing, they gather to hold it, again with one thought. One intention.

"It's good," they gesture, encircling all space above and

around with a wave of arm, slowly turning their sleek bodies in a full circle and looking up.

Standing together, they call for strength in pacts made before earth and sky, binding these in songs and prayers. Hailing forces in ground and air, camps overflow with other people open to their way of continuance. Flashes of those gatherings whisk by. Flame becomes flame and Lily closes her eyes. Waiting.

Trails leading here…

Flicking fire makes her look to it once more, at long-ago life revealing itself there, radiant, aglow.

⇅

Revelation… It came to a woman… A WOMAN… They say…

Among her own people, she was always one of them. Growing up, she merged easily into any group of children, young people, and women, vanishing there, shielded in camp life and by the earth's cloak as moons died and were reborn, and snows softly sifted down to become other things, sinking into or rising off the ground.

All the while, she was part of that, new moons and pelting snow, yet was becoming more herself, more distinct each season, going into maturity, toward destiny.

Late one sun, out she stepped from earlier seasons of invisibility and stood clear in the foreground of that place; mingled sights and sounds of her people moving about filled her up and she responded. An echo of children's voices rose behind a string of tipis where small boys played on both sides of narrow swishing water, and other voices bubbled at its edge, floating under budding trees with new bark. There, she listened to the voice of each thing; evening light cast upon her. Not too young or old either, she walked toward her brother's tipi standing on a smooth rise of pale green surrounded by fragrant ground, and her life turned.

His tipi was distinct, marked with vibrant streaks of color. His youthful wife greeted her. "Horses," she said, indicating nearby corrals but motioning to a place beside her.

Soon, a tall blue silhouette separated from sinuous drifts of orange haze. Gait and torso were recognizable.

Come! He beckoned. She followed a circle he cut around camp, walking deliberately at turtle's pace, noting everything. Clouds ascending, pulling away, breaking apart, fading. Wet plants pushing out on banks. Figures moving to and from narrow trickling water. Motion on land. Swirling in sky. Piercing calls in trees, flicking grass.

His walk, physique, and voice held no hint of old age, but face to face, his long braided hair slightly laced dark and silver threads and fine scratches encircled his brown eyes and his set mouth. The depth of his eyes, shrewd eyes, revealed maturity and flinty hardness, experience acquired only in deadly battles, and from witnessing strong men fall, not to rise again.

With night hovering, they returned to his tipi. He said "Sister! Four suns shall cross. Twelve men shall depart then. South, they'll ride, toward barren, rough ground far away. To a place of scarcity. Over there, water sometimes conceals itself as do plants and game. Nearly one moon's cycle shall pass. Then our travelers shall arrive."

His voice, full of gravel from streambeds the people had followed and drank in earliest times, he kept down so as not to disturb darkness and meditation darkness brings. She leaned in to hear.

"Sister!" his voice dropped even more, "Lead! They said. For you have led before! They said that to me. And I agreed! Now we prepare.

"Younger brother, who just joined our camp, will come with us. We'll take one boy to care for horses. We'll be gone awhile. At a long distance.

"All agreed, because of time and distance, a woman may be willing to help."

Silence. Space. Her eyes found the smoke hole as they always did at that time; up there, two shiny flints began to spark.

That woman... A stranger... Mysterious yet so clear...

Old age! Her people claimed of those flints as they looked upward. Then she said, "Brother, I've heard of it. That place. Never do women go there! Never do women travel with men this way!" Her voice was as low as his, thoughtful, steady.

"I'm alone, now. Still I have two brothers here—and an older sister and another brother in other camps. Our mother, our father, now all-spirit, advised me as a child to help brothers and sisters. Be helpful! That's what they said. You know me. I'm strong. With my youngest child, I'll go—to help. My child and I won't be separated!"

Her brother's arms folded; he accepted her response.

"Three new moons, maybe four, will pass. For that long, we'll be away from here. Dear sister! It's a rough trail. We never undertake it lightly." He held up both hands, palms facing her and paused. Their identical eyes met, gauging each other in dim light.

His were direct then and their lightning effect made her reel. Warning!

"Nephew should stay with you. All the time! Six winters, that's too early to help in ways needed out there. Stay in camp when we arrive. Both of you will surely be safe."

A woman with a child...

A woman with brothers...

Older brother as leader was not new. She and her children were always in his hands. Both brothers alone held many of the people that way through previous snows.

"He goes," she repeated.

Older brother continued. "The names of the travelers are..."

Lily's eyes settle on her own brother, sitting on the ground near the tipi door. He had started the fire. His eyes are shut and his back is straight but relaxed.

Man's nature... Woman's nature...

Leaving her brother's tipi, camp lay under an ascending, swelling moon, brighter outside than in the tipi. Drifting clouds gave off shell white luster, lit by the glow of the strolling moon. Behind these were bright sparks. Rustling wind over the narrow stream nudged her. She passed her own empty tipi and went on to younger brother's place. He was outside, poking a few live coals. Her son slept nearby.

Leave him! He gestured.

Then he asked so quietly, "Did brother tell you?"

"Yes, I and this boy will go along with all of you."

He patted her hand and then he became silence.

Back in her own tipi and settling down, rest didn't come. Her mind leapt to the next sun and to tasks for a long journey to an unknown place.

A deep booming voice announced it to the entire camp at first light. As news went through, a bustle of activity began. As for her, she collected and prepared dry foods, and went in search of material for extra moccasins and clothing for herself, her child, brothers and other men.

Next, she rummaged in a small supply of herbs for minor ailments. What she didn't have was traded or given to her.

"Surely, you will need this," others offered, bringing an assortment of things. When everyone left, she wrapped and sorted items, so they wouldn't be lost or forgotten.

She chose two hides for herself and two for her child for protection and bed. At the end of three suns those few things were stored in a manageable bundle. A small pack was for her child. She awaited the next sun curiously.

Early, camp came to life. Younger brother led two horses her way, one already laced with packs. She climbed on the other after he secured her packs to it. She recognized the errand boy, of about thirteen winters, who would tend horses. Her child laughed and recognized him, "Bone! Bone!"

He stood beside her child. Both of them, eager to start, nudged each other in anticipation.

"Nephew stays with you," younger brother said. "Lively horses! Too lively for him!" He lifted the boy behind her.

"Returning, he might ride with me," he said leaving, followed by Bone.

Under a handful of flints still glinting dimly above, the two waited on horseback, nearly unseen on great gentle swells and slightly breathing ground. Her mind stored everything as her child called to other boys. He was all arms and legs.

The profile of Lily's brother is highlighted by low orange blaze as he turns a smoky log.

Brother seems to be part of the story... Part of memory...

She kissed her village, ground and sky known from birth, inhaling deeply to draw them inside her flesh and bones. It was moist and grassy fragrance she inhaled, along with the scent of the warm horse.

Grass was ankle-high, thick, wet, rope like. Her people were scarcely there — faint enough in thin veiled light that they may not have been solid, were spirits in dreams.

East, a band of light peeked over the edge of creeping ground. Northward, a small forest swayed. Right then it was barely distinct from lingering night. West, below camp, the narrow winding stream gently trickled over slippery mossy stones. Overhead, a pale wash began to flood empty sky, spreading up and outward. Birds began to cheep and other wild things lifted their heads, stealthily raking thick wet grass.

Her small tipi stood in the care of relatives. Side by side, they were in front of it, waving to her and her child, riding out behind the men. The horse was going effortlessly under her and her child was talking. Bone was last, leading an extra horse. Around them earth fanned out in soft billowing swells, and above, sky was infinitely spacious, wide open, and they rode into it.

They went purposefully southward without eating and with no talk. She kept pace, staying back. Now and then her child showed a burst of energy, brushing against her or turning towards Bone, still riding behind. Once in a while, one brother swooped out from others ahead and rode alongside, he and the child making signs to one another.

As sun dipped down, two of their group galloped away, returning with small game. Before dusk, they stopped to sleep. She welcomed it. Her body was pulled, stretched.

First, one man started a blaze and soon smoking fur was pungent in sweet air. Shortly, they ate and claimed places to sleep. All the men kept a clear distance from her, addressing her as a relative. In turn, she responded. She placed her and her child's bed near younger brother.

Sky descended, rippling and flexing, and she felt its greatness. Drifting into sleep, her presence there jolted her awake again.

Rarely would a woman be along. When it happened, men changed their ways.

What they altered, she couldn't say. She only knew that they traveled without a holy man to advise them on steps of war and peace. The oldest member of their group was beyond fifty winters, older brother. Younger groups carried along old men to ensure success and safety, but in theirs, all were experienced in ways of the world.

Unlikely as it was, here she was with warrior men, fearsome men who reached out and touched death daily to discover what it was and what they were.

When she fell asleep, their voices were muffled, planning the next sun's campsite, recalling good places to water and rest horses, and trails to follow. Just before her eyes closed, their watchman moved a step from where he stood, to one side. He was utter silence, but he moved.

Woman's place... Man's place... Peace... War...

‡v

Footfalls of horses... Footfalls...

Each sun was a hot glow in soft empty folds of sky. Then light smudges appeared and warm spray. The only woman there looked up, opening her mouth to swallow the clear drops, but they were few, gone before their smudges faded away.

Older brother pushed everyone. After a while, they entered new space where the dampness of their homeland no longer soaked their clothing and coated their skin, and swatches of blue sky no longer dropped down to surround them in colorful mists or became swirls to other worlds, as happened back there. Too, lulls came in ever present but sometimes nearly undetectable surges of abundant streams and rivers crisscrossing the ground; wide lush curving hills holding bones of their ancestors fell silently behind.

Older brother held up a hand. On that border he looked back where they had been, and then at her.

"Get your bearings. Renew yourself."

They stayed the night and the next, and all the men rode a short distance away without explanation the next dawn. They moved about over there while the horses grazed and wind carried gray puffs of smoke and an odor of sweet herbs to her, but she didn't see or know more than that.

Resuming their ride, stretches of tall fragrant grass thinned, then disappeared. New shrubs and other grassy cover poked up from rocky soil. There was a change in the sound of the land, an absence of water trickling and rumbles in the sky. Her child leaned against her and said, "Look down! What grows...."

"And what of all this is food?" she wondered.

In stony ravines, white mice whisked lightly under them. Rocks rolled down one at a time from narrow sidewalls extending overhead. They broke the stillness. Now and then, a surprised coyote turned and ran, then stopped to watch them pass, its furry silhouette glowing in the light. Details.

Despite a steady pace, her boy showed good nature, boundless energy and curiosity of young everywhere.

Older brother made two more, longer stops, first at a large shiny black lake with marshy, spongy sides, and next at a gurgling stream. The horses were released at the lake and ventured in, splashing and churning black water as the men refilled the water bags. Around the lake was mud that pulled the horses down into it. Each sun thereafter, water holes were further apart and shallow. A stretch of land came into view where only tall wispy brush and prickly plants thrived, and in spots, hard crusty earth lay completely exposed as far as eyes saw. Sometimes, bright grainy sand blinded them. Each sun set off hot dry blasts, but nights became cool. In the distance, a line of low dark jagged mountains cut upward.

Older brother proved himself daily. His small group always located water, old and new springs, though sometimes they all dug in rocks and clay and waited until the clouds in the water cleared.

Once, four of them rode off, shortly returning with refilled water bags and refreshed horses. The men praised that place, remembering how far they still had to go. Two scouts went on to find other springs ahead and to search for other people. They met no one, but were close enough to see where others had just been, soft tracks in the land.

Lily's eyes study clean swept ground in the tipi, its contour and grainy texture in firelight, and she feels a comforting human hand. Stark contrast to wide open unknown spaces.

Yet it's the same ground... The same mama...

∨

Generations... Different peoples... Different histories...

She and her child got down from their horse. The boy darted forward, flapping his arms, as boys do when set loose. Her eyes swept over unknown terrain and then went north, imagining her tipi far beyond. Spent suns and a long road they came had vanished. Older brother had taken them from their flat lands, shown them distant mountains and valleys, and brought them down steep inclines. Unable to recall the whole way, she saw the stranger she was here. Only sparking flints in the spirit world were what she knew for sure.

Pulling a scratchy stem from a shrub, she sniffed it. Both brothers approached; each scuffled with her child.

Older brother pointed, "Two suns! We'll arrive. Camp. Below this pass."

Closer but still distant were peaks earlier seen. Sky was lighter gray than the mountains; sun's brightness was veiled.

"You are fit?" he asked though she stood lean, strong. Continuous riding had toughened her. Her body flexed and she leaped right at him, playfully.

Evening filled with men's stories of the gorge they were entering and of other journeys there. Two nights had been darker and deeper; in that depth two new flints lit in the south when she lay down.

As older brother foretold, he put camp on a slope with a view of all directions. Here, the voice of the land was different, again. Feathery bushes whipped and bobbed in small frenzied dust storms. As these lashed, a spin of lavender and green lizards and brown snakes darted out when men began to repair two shelters there. Her child laughed at those lightning streaks as he raced with them, calling.

"It takes knowing people to live in places like this," she told him and mentioned a couple of old stories of the harshest places their people had been.

Hidden in rocky ridges, camp was protected from severe winds whistling afar. She skirted the area and outlines of previous camps were evident in each direction.

The string of horses was led to a natural enclosure away from camp and she asked younger brother, "Water?"

He pointed in the opposite direction.

"How far?"

"Right here. It's almost gone. Too soon it will dry unless rain forms. Have no fear, sister! We, too, will be far from here."

She then fashioned a bed for herself and her child to share. Though the place was unknown, the two were in the care of her brothers, and night was untroubled, full of peace.

Soft... Restoring..

VȈ

Peace... War... Daily life...

The men took off noisily at sunrise, riding out in three directions, their horses stamping ground. She and her child, and Bone, stood in an unsettling stillness afterward. Later she realized it visited after each sunrise.

She followed Bone as he led the horses, one at a time, to water. He and her child were ahead, laughing, talking. They all climbed the ridge pointed out by younger brother. The snorting horse alerted her to the pool.

Two arroyos met and formed a small shallow basin filled by flash floods running into that bowl. The place was marked with indications of recent rain, maybe six or seven suns before. Deep gouges cut crumbling purple clay. She also saw why her brother hadn't put camp closer. Tracks of animals and birds pressed into its edges, disappearing on a rocky shelf above the pool. Some she didn't know. There was no cover from loud torrential wind swooping down the slopes, flinging water out, drying the pool bit by bit. Water spit at them; strong red spray hit her child's face, left it dotted with red blotches. He and Bone laughed at his spattered face, but she turned away.

Camp was quiet until the others returned. After tending their horses, each group described what lay in the direction taken, and their reports made her curious. The first group said, "Not far away, enemy people! A strange group. Their language makes ringing sounds." Another told, "Salt water sits over there. At the base of low mountains laying to the east." All of them looked eastward where the mountains were haze. The third group spoke of empty settlements abandoned for many seasons. After older brother voiced his plan for the next sun, it was her turn to feed everyone and help anyone who asked.

Older brother added as she moved away, "We'll take Bone tomorrow and all the horses."

She nodded.

When the men left the next sun, she and her child began to explore the outlying country.

Women as seekers... What calls us?

Two white suns ran overhead; the men returned. They talked excitedly, ate, slept, and departed again. Altogether, for a string of suns, life went that way.

"Sister!" older brother told her before he left the last time, "Two suns will pass. Before the second is gone, we'll return. Then to our homeland we'll go."

She was satisfied. Her tipi waited.

He added, "Hereabouts are enemy people. We've met them before. They know us! But you'll be safe here."

"What kind of people are they?" she asked.

"Suspicious!" he answered. "They suspect everyone not belonging to them. In appearance, they don't use clothing such as ours. Loose capes and coverings wrap their limbs. That's what they wear. Their ways are angry, too!"

Bone left smiling, happy to be included. All rode noisily away, the youngest waving at her child and leading the two extra horses, trailing the others. Flying sand chased them.

Later with her child leaping ahead, she went out in an unexplored direction. Only striking muted colors, layers of light, were there and they drew her into them. Where she stood, nothing grew. Large birds soared back and forth hypnotically until their squawking hacked the placid sky. Then a wind fluttered gently, keeping on until nightfall, building up, and spinning harshly around the shelter and into rocky crevices around camp, and in it were high mournful sounds.

Later, she told of raw power there; she felt its wildness, its truth.

VII

The men failed to come back.

Shading her eyes with a hand, she scoured the hot horizon. That night she strained to hear horses strike ground. Rising up often because she wanted to be awake when they came in, she slept lightly. When night was nearly gone, eagerly she stood on the highest nearby ridge, watching. Waiting. In the east, sun's power showed bare hills, infinite empty ridges.

Two more suns rolled so slowly overhead, in them was a strum of ancient rousing, the very beginning of everything. Those two paused directly above, hanging indefinitely, before settling into hazy foothills stretching out that way. Waiting, she and her boy retraced the way the men rode out, going as far as they could. She halted, facing the unknown. Nothing in sight moved except noisy birds turning, twirling, in a vast blue dome. Low ranging ridges to the northeast, the way back, were more distant, more desolate, each time they went out.

Out there the boy stopped and questioned her, "Where are they?" His face tilted up. He shared the features of her brothers.

"Anytime, they'll ride in." She was uncertain and used stories to distract him.

Another sun passed, and another. Those two crept ever more slowly across endless space, stretching the limits of her being. Again, during their passing, she and her child walked out to search for human movement, but they had no luck. Those nights when she lay down, the sparking flints were reassuring. Pictures of her tipi and her people's camps, and their laughter and soothing voices were close and far. How she missed them! Restless as she was, her eyes popped open at windy noise and night's tiniest scratching, waiting for light.

When it burst forth, she was exhausted. She looked at her still-sleeping child beside her, tenderly stroked his face and hair.

She rose and looked northward, at the pass older brother brought them through; she guessed it was a walk of maybe four suns. Between camp and the pass was waterless.

She was torn. The pool had sifted up and blown away. If they had water or could find it, they might stay.

Sky was cloudy, dull gray, exuding its early stillness. She wanted rain. That miracle happened even there, but too soon, ground glared. She had to blink at rising heat. As best she could tell from her perch on the ridge, water was a long ride north, or a sun's ride east, according to what her brothers said. She wasn't sure how far it would be on foot. She didn't know the exact location of water in the east either; she hadn't listened very well to the men's stories.

"I should have listened better!" she scolded herself.

How many times in life do we say that? The same words...

As she stood there, her son asked pointedly, "Are my uncles coming back?"

She hadn't heard him rise. "I don't know," she confessed.

They looked at each other deeply, down to their hearts.

"We have food to last for maybe six suns." She had already started to fast the day the men didn't return. "But we need water."

Life came down to it.

Water...

Wind filtered through the crags, whistling.

"Shall we go back?" she asked unexpectedly.

"Just us?" he asked in surprise.

He looked at her with a shadow in his eyes, but she met them, and nodded. After surveying their empty camp, his shoulders dropped and he agreed.

What's childhood without purity and trust? Those turn so fast...

viii

Who really knows for certain what she will do in unforeseen events life brings? Each of us thinks she knows...

Still wishful, she waited for sun to descend. Then she untied a shriveled water bag, and wrapped their remaining food into a tiny bundle. She picked up one of older brother's blankets, looping food, water, and the thin blanket around her body, and she placed a smaller bedroll on her child's back.

Without a backward glance she chose a way out on one side explored earlier, her child leaping into her tracks.

She walked, wishing for her brothers. "Surely, if they draw breath, they will return!" Hope steadied her.

Mother and son walked in an erratic pace until dusk.

The child ran or straggled as he wished. They could have walked all night if she knew the way but they lay down in a wide open space.

Night wind on lower, flatter, ground was desolate, sweeping in images of all the missing men and the trail she had to make to her people, alone.

Before sunrise, she pulled on her child to wake him, and they began to walk without taking water or food. When sun reached its full strength, they stopped, sinking down beside the only brush in sight, stinging needles as high as her knees. In the south was their camp, too far away to be seen, but barely behind them. Closing her eyes for a while, her child had time and more than enough energy to chase lizards and tiny birds over mounds of glistening sand. When sun crawled more westward and she was cooled, they took up their journey again.

She began to lose count of suns. By and by, the boy became hungrier and more tired, and his high whining voice was out of place in the deep quiet there.

"We could go faster on a horse!" he said. She nodded her head vigorously in agreement. "It's far....," he added.

She hugged him and selected songs and stories to soothe them and to diminish their pangs of hunger. On they went, at an even slower pace. By then her sense of sun's journey had altered. *Sun rises. Sun goes down. Sun rises. Sun stands still.* When it appeared to stop movement altogether, she forced herself forward.

Walking she accepted. Her people walked all their known country countless times.

That night, her child sleeping soundly, she looked up and spoke to the rippling power above. "If we had food, water and fire! If we could sit inside my own tipi and all my beloved were there!" Overcome with longing, she gave a heart wrenching sob before blackness above shuddered in shimmering sparks and the faces of her brothers and the other men looked at her from way up there.

Lily leans back against the tipi pole and its solidity brings her back to present.

Grief... Loneliness...

The next sun her child drank the last of their water. He gulped it greedily and then met his mother's eyes. Her hand dipped into the last of their food, enough to fill one palm, and she offered it to him.

"It's gone?" he asked.

They were dust, their faces raw from blasting wind.

The sun was still bearable. They went on without incident. If she only knew the way!

The high rocky pass guided her. Looking to that again, there was flickering in the distance. Rainbow heat rose; afterward, she thought her eyes played tricks. She and her child kept walking. Suddenly it appeared again!

"Watch!" she pointed toward colored beams hovering in the distance. Sun's hottest time. She looked for shelter and concealment. They spied a depression in the hillside.

"What's that?" she pointed after settling on her stomach on searing hot ground. They peered through short scraggly brush.

They tried to locate movement again. Her son spotted it first, a wavy blur, far away. Soon, the line advanced.

"Men," her son said.

"My uncles are returning!" he said excitedly, his voice rising. He scrambled to stand.

"No," she whispered, pulling him down. "Your uncles are on horseback."

Both pushed further down into the shallow depression and she hoped they were shielded.

The stranger people looked like they were coming directly at them. She wanted another place to better hide but there wasn't any.

Spread out in burning sun as the two of them were, the approach of the strangers went slowly. Mother and son tensed; their bodies were jumpy. Sweat beads formed above swollen brown lips and across their foreheads and rolled into their eyes. Insects hummed in their ears.

Her son's parched lips silently formed "Enemies!" as if the men out there would catch his thoughts.

Finally, they heard the strangers, barely. Her son's lips moved again in a crawling motion, "Hear?" They listened curiously. Cautiously.

His eyes locked on the men as he pushed a small shoulder against hers. Their backs burned.

The strangers talked freely, moving forward hurriedly.

"Can they help?" she asked herself.

Closer, the strangers were visible. They wore light garments. Across their shoulders and between their legs draped loose coverings. Feathers hung from caps, and flicked in hot breeze. They carried weapons. Wooden and metal clubs. Metal flashed.

Her child waited questioningly. She put one hand over her mouth and one over his. Hot steam seeped through her fingers. They turned face to face, looking into each other's eyes.

She made herself flat, part of the ground beside her child's body, one arm holding him down firmly as the line of strangers passed. She stopped breathing. Her child, too, exhaled and she felt thumps inside him.

The strangers passed, stopped, inspecting the ground. One wandered in their direction, pausing. The rest went on, calling him back.

Mother and child lay there until those threatening voices left and the mirage floated away. When sun lost its burn, and she regained courage, she put her child ahead. "Lead!" she indicated.

Without food or water, she was wildly desperate and looked back longingly several times in the direction the strangers went. Into darkness, she and the boy moved northward. Finally, just below the pass, they threw themselves down. He was asleep right away. Up in the rocks they would climb the next sun she heard animals howl and scurry. She tried to stay awake to protect them, but her eyes clamped tight against her will.

When she woke, sun was already high, and her body was stiff, stone-heavy. Large boulders were strewn around her; rats' nests filled crevices in the boulders and way up the craggy ridge rested empty bird nests and droppings. Thirsty, hungry, and feeling very weak, she forced herself to sit up.

Her child sat on a massive boulder above, his legs dangling. Looking down, he calmly observed her.

She said, "We've lost the coolest time."

"In your sleep, you talked and cried." His face was dark and dry.

"Are we lost?" he asked.

"No," she answered. "When we cross this, we'll see for sure."

In shadows of steep inclines, they slowly climbed. When sun descended halfway, they were nearly through the pass. There, another stretch of dry land awaited, less dismal than where they'd been. Birds circled and screeched. Ahead grew more kinds of plants and scattered tufts of grass. Surely, some of it was food! Water was here. Her heart was happier at the sight. The way through it was unknown but the two were this much closer to their own people.

All that promise was quickly knocked away by whipping wind, beating on them soon after they came out that side. It grew fiercer when they stopped to find a route down. Turning away from that threatening force, she put up her arms to shield herself.

"Truly, I don't know where we are, or this side better than the other!" she shrieked. Her words flung back to her along with slinging sand and whirling wind filled her ears.

Her child didn't hear. His hair blew straight back away from his face as he squinted to see. He held a hand over his eyes, spitting sand. Wind was loud, furious. His small body leaned forward into those thrusts.

Forces of earth and sky... All of story...

She tried to recall their journey southward. Thought didn't stay. Wind slapped it out of her. Her body grew more weighty and clumsy. She couldn't see in the dust. How she wanted water! How tired she was!

Her child, stronger than she, thin and limber, bent into wind. He looked back at her, yelling something she couldn't hear.

Her memory was wiped clean. Where was she? She saw herself back where her brother left her and was startled out of that by hurling wind, spinning sand. She willed her legs to move.

Her body desired water. Her mouth was too dry. The men had told where water was and she had been near it. She wasn't able to lift her feet and legs anymore. She wanted to stop and sit down.

Wind thrust frantically. She was sweating and her body was too warm. She tried shaking off the sick feeling, fixing her gaze on her child's small figure in front of her.

He set a pace for her however light her head and heavy her feet. She was capable of floating; still her feet stayed on the ground, stumbling, following the child she was born to protect.

Down the pass they slowly made way. They were creeping along like that when wind quieted and her child finally turned around in that sudden calmness.

"Which way did your uncles come?" she asked in a daze. "Do you remember?"

He shrugged helplessly. "I don't know!"

She was off balance. Bracing herself, she toppled in front of him anyway.

He leaned over her. "What's wrong?"

She looked frightening. Glazed eyes made her fearsome.

"How long have we been walking? Six suns? Seven?" Her words were slow, thick.

He sat down beside her, resting a small hand on her. He didn't try to answer. She felt wild, no longer like herself.

"Can you go on alone?" she asked. "I might not help anymore. I can't keep up. You're strong. If you must, go on by yourself. Find water. Then go home."

His mouth dropped open; she saw his surprise.

"You can do it," she said more gently.

"Home?" he repeated. "I don't want to go without you."

He pulled and tugged on her, trying to force her up. Wearily she lifted herself, took a few steps before slipping down.

Taking off the thin bedroll, he asked, "Which way is water? Which way? I'll get it for you. Where is it?"

She heard. Her eyes looked upward at something far away and then closed. Still, she heard him. He sat beside her for a while, motionless. Then, he set out to find water.

He returned empty handed but saw mice and other

things. She looked asleep; he tried shaking her. It did no good. She couldn't respond.

Huddling down beside her on bare ground, flints begin to spark above. His mother appeared lifeless; he kept on talking anyway. He wanted to help but tiredness overcame him. His mouth was cracked and his stomach sounded hungry.

Mothers and sons... Generations...

IX

Birth... Death... Joy... Fear...

Her body was numb; her lips parched. Her child hailed from afar. She heard him beg, Water! She was sad because she had none to give. Dusky blue-black space was all there was. Not even flints sparked. Dark space extended everywhere, a sweeping overpowering force. Churning and deep, it whisked light and sound into it, creating a deafening roar.

She lay in that for an unknowable time, trying to will her body to move, to speak. She was stuck, paralyzed. Then an inner self gently parted from her stiff reclining body, flying up gracefully out of it. That self was whole, weightless, and had glorious lightning movement. It knew what to do. Did she dream?

She was on a glossy plane moving effortlessly and saw herself asleep on the ground, her son curled at one side. Light as a sparrow, she felt freedom never known before.

Nearby, a mist of light began to spin and pulsate. A soft fan of pastel colors burst open there, shooting upward, tinting space. Effortlessly she moved toward that. Coming up on it, she saw a figure sitting in the center of light. Clear beams of rainbow colors emanated from him. How wondrous he was! He looked at her, gesturing, beckoning.

She responded timidly and yet willingly; her birdlike heart and self tingled in his presence. She heard a voice, his voice, but he didn't speak in her way.

Daughter!

What you need is here!

Medicine!

Nourishment!

Strength! Endurance!

This will show you the way home!

Unexpectedly, he sprung into a standing position, as if he, too, had power of flight. Beneath, and all around him, a plant in various sizes and shapes pushed out of rocky soil.

Daughter, take these!

They will help!

They will care for you!

Before she could reply, that radiant pastel light softened, diffused. The wonderful being of light faded before her eyes.

But then hundreds of flinty sparks appeared and trembled around her. Trembled. She moved effortlessly toward her sleeping body, gazing down at it. Suddenly, she was inside it again, feeling its weighty trunk and her limbs. She draped her arms across her stomach. She felt warm wind inside herself.

Divine universe…

X

Her story… From her own lips… Other versions… On and on…

Dawn. Her child tugged; his face was alarmed. When she opened her eyes, he was so relieved he squealed.

"I can't find water!" he admitted. "Can you walk?"

She tried to move, sat up with his help. Then he pulled her arms. Unable to rise fast enough to suit him, he was miserable again.

She clasped his small hand, stroking it. "We've come this far," she said, more herself than last night, "through waterless land and rocky pass. We must eat now, or surely go into the spirit world."

Her words made her examine the surrounding landscape, a certain direction.

"Let's go up there. Help me!"

He tugged and pushed her.

"You're too heavy!" He was breathless.

Finally she stood on her own, swaying. Her forehead was covered in sweaty beads and she flung them off.

Step by step, they climbed. Just before reaching the top, a wave of cold darkness blocked her vision. It passed and her sight cleared. Sun sat on a higher knoll behind the one they climbed, throwing bright streaks at many plants barely peeking from the ground.

"There!" she called, "There!"

She let go the child's hand, got down on her knees.

"What?" he asked.

She dug around a tiny plant with her fingers, scraping back dirt, first slowly and then rapidly but it was deeply rooted in hard soil.

"Help!" she called again.

He knelt beside her, trying to dig one side while she uncovered the other. They tugged. Using a sharp edge of stone, they dug until the plant loosened. It was longer than wide, as round as the tip of her thumb, a soft sage color at the top, with sections to it. A moist green layer was under the skin of the plant where the stone punctured it. She brushed off grains of sand pressed into its surface.

She took a bite, ground her teeth on sand and tasted juicy tartness. Swallowing was hard with her mouth so dry. "Bitter!" she said. Breaking off a section, she offered that to her child. He took it without question, biting into it and wrinkling his face.

They ate three or four plants, wiping sand and grit from each, and picking at a white tuft on the top.

She dug out a few more plants, laying them aside. Her fingers were torn. She brushed off dots of blood.

Those few bites began to fill their hunger and satisfy their thirst.

"I'll sleep now," she told him. "We'll stay here. Look for water. Bring the bedroll."

All the plants nearly hid themselves completely in the ground. When her child brought the bedding, she made a shade amongst them. She was asleep when her head touched ground. Morning was still cool.

Seeing she was stronger, beginning to look and sound like herself, the boy played nearby, watching her sleep until sun was directly overhead.

When she woke, they ate plants put aside earlier. Fatigue was letting go of her, and her aching body slightly soothed. That day her child noted a line of moisture, and fine moss on the side of a nearby ridge, where he later took her.

They stayed in that garden three or four suns in very little cover. Sleeping often as she needed, she grew stronger while the boy became playful again. She dreamed one dream again and again: she sitting and walking in a garden with a rainbow being who spoke kindly to her.

Each sun revived her strength and courage, and she and her child dug plants, using tools they made to lift them out of the ground. That work took much effort to dig only a few. She was patient. When she thought they had enough, she split the plants between them, carrying them as they could, and headed on.

Soon a trickle of water was heard.

"Life!" she said, soaking the shriveled water bag in the tiny gleaming stream. "This is life!"

Then they killed small animals, things they hadn't ever eaten.

Living off plants they carried, and her vivid dreams, they finally arrived at broad swatches of grassland and an abundance of crisscrossing shiny streams. Purely by chance, they crossed the wider and deeper ones. Later, the soil softened into lush damp hillsides and the whole sky was theirs again, behaving in its familiar way, fully wrapping them in colorful mists and fogs and then dissolving at will.

Occasionally they nearly met others, but the two went around them, avoiding contact.

On a joyful evening there they were, on the border of their land. Late next sun they entered camp moved from the earlier place, because that was how their people marked seasonal change. Barking dogs and neighing horses announced them. Her child called out excitedly, "We have returned! We have come home!"

Relatives rushed to greet them, holding them tightly and happily in the curve of their arms, a hush falling when relatives understand no others were with them and mother and child were on foot.

"They are alone!" the crowd repeated among themselves.

He who was now called Leader stepped forward.

"What has happened?"

Her brother's young wife made her way toward them and stood close, her face guarded, a hand clutching the child's shoulders before the hands of old women led him away.

"Three moons have died since our group of fifteen left our camp, going south." She recounted events in the expected way, without haste, and with attention to details. She described much, the land they passed through and what someone in the group had said at a certain time. She went through each moon, up to when she and her boy left that far away shelter. In her telling, tears slid down her face when she spoke of the men whose absence she could not explain.

She held her people's attention briefly. Then families of the missing men began to gather and speak among themselves.

Older brother's wife walked silently away.

When excitement of their homecoming settled, and news of missing men went out to the entire camp and beyond, and a plan was made to discover what had happened to them, the new leader sought her out and sat with her.

"Tell me," he finally asked, "how did you found your way back? From such a distant, unknown place?"

It was then she brought out plants she had carried, placing them before him. They were dry and hard.

"With these..."

He examined them.

"If not for these, we would not be here! We would not have lived! We would not have come back!" She told him of the plants she was shown and of the garden she had seen.

Sacred ground...

Lily closes her eyes, thinks of that woman who is now long gone. Few people knew her, or heard her story from her own lips, but that story had its own life. To the farthest reaches of this land it went.

Now it had unwound again like a long strap, distant from where it happened, four or five generations earlier. Present to past.

At the end of the story Lily sees herself sitting in the tipi and she draws a deep breath at where that humble woman's experience led. Past to present.

Story's way... Fire flicking, flicking...

The tipi curves around Lily; she sits in its embrace. Fire dances in the center, bringing comfort. She rises, looks around. Everything is here. Everything is in order. Waiting.

Sanctuary...

PART TWO

Melting Snow

Midnight song

Recorded by Kish Hawkins

Cody

First time he picked up medicine was a long time ago—in the 1930s—when it made its way west. Afterward, he was outside the law for a while simply by accepting the new ceremony.

I don't forget it...

One breezy sundown he rode horseback with Little Man up to a secluded *hogan* in the *Lukachukai* mountains to see what it was really about. He'd heard enough second-hand and went up there to discover truth for himself.

He and Little Man were faint jostling figures riding quietly into blue folds of the soft looming mountain. They didn't talk like some do.

Earth and sky speak... It's enough...

Winter showed up early that year, gliding down from dark peaks farther north. Dry brown oak leaves felt the freeze first, dropping slowly down into crunchy slippery beds making up forest ground. Cody pulled his faded wool jacket a little closer with a gloved hand in blasts of icy air, tucking his jutting chin further down into the fleecy collar; its fabric stretched taut across his shoulders and around his forearms. His hat brushed the collar now and then, and that occasional brushing was about all he heard on the ride up.

Our trail spiraled from ground to sky... Ahead our path was twilight...

An early star hung over tall fragrant pines. Wind sifted through them, making raspy sounds. Limbs whisked Cody's shoulder with their needles and scent as the horses wound around.

He followed Little Man until pale amber lights bobbed ahead.

Someone greeted, "Put the horses in the corral."

Cody and Little Man climbed off in early starlight and slung their saddles over the fence where a few horses snorted and bunched together on one side, their eyes gleaming in thickening dusk. Behind them forest and sky were spacious. Beyond that was something even more limitless.

The figure greeting them moved around a woodpile, picking up an armload of firewood and carrying it inside. Soon the same husky figure led Cody and Little Man into a small *hogan* where an oil lamp burned weakly on the north side in front of a tiny low window, casting dingy light on gathered curtains. Only a handful of people were there.

It started out that way...

Crossed logs marked the center of the dwelling. There, a young man made a quiet skinny stream of faint blue smoke rise; flame came alive in an abrupt high leap, cracking, popping. A spray of tiny orange sparks shot up in little arches before sprinkling cold ground. As it grew brighter, indistinguishable shapes of people separated from dusky log walls, visibly softer and more rounded. Before that, they were shadowy lumps against the wall. Cody didn't recognize anyone. A stranger on the west side who used foreign speech, sounds of *bilagaana* language, was not familiar at all.

I never use foreign language... Though I know hello, good-bye, and ho-kay...

All his life he avoided foreign words because they were clumsy on his tongue, and didn't sound right in his own ears, and earlier as a boy when he used them, someone near him broke into a wide grin, eyes twinkling mischievously.

The stranger gestured toward himself, saying quite a bit. He sat on dirt, with lower legs crossed in front of him, heels tucked under his thighs. Indian was the only word Cody understood. The stranger paused a few seconds to let it sink in but Cody already knew from the stranger's bones and skin, the way he sat and his unmistakable hand gestures. Then the stranger pointed to the fire, the *hogan* walls, the ground and smoke hole before saying more.

Someone brought store tobacco to Cody and Little Man and they rolled smokes while the stranger used an interpreter and sometimes threw in a word from Cody's own language, though awkward and unclear.

He began, "My relatives, I traveled far to carry something good out here. I did it because it's what you said you wanted."

I was mindful though I didn't know his words...

Later, someone told them to Cody and described how slowly the stranger talked because the language he used wasn't really his either.

A poker passed to light all the smokes in the circle and then the stranger said his first prayer that night. He prayed in two languages, switching back and forth. Cody sucked on his smoke, its tip glowing bright orange in his long fingers. Afterwards, smokes were collected and medicine went around the circle. That's how it all began, this part of Cody's story.

Forty-six winters behind me...... Melted snow now.... Two, three generations...

The stranger lifted a long wooden staff in his left hand and held a gourd rattle in his right. The rattle swished. Swished. Swished. The weight of his body balanced on his left knee; his right leg was bent and his knee extended outward. He was fairly young, too, maybe between thirty and forty winters.

At the stranger's right, an older man began to beat on a black iron kettle drum, filled with water, when the rattle came to life. The log walls, earthen roof, and ground muffled strikes on the drum. The stranger sang in a deeper voice than his speaking one, yet his song rose pleasantly from the west wall. Cody didn't know what the song said or hadn't heard any other like it.

A couple of old men prayed individually between songs sung by the stranger and others. Their language and groaning bodies reminded him of all the shapes and forms life took to fully express itself. One at a time, the old men's voices cracked and broke open, full of breathy sounds and emotion. Their speech described long lives and an expected share of rough times.

The first rearranged his brittle body, straightening his back as best he could, and prayed on bony knees for a long time. His words were husky, rising and falling, rising and falling, creating a pool of emotion around him like frothy ripples spinning and rushing down the San Juan River during a heavy drizzle.

The second old man's speech traveled out on its own in a remarkably visible way after he composed himself to pray. In that long prayer of fervent pauses followed by rushing streams of words, the old man described Cody's life as well as his own, though they had only spoken to each other previously no more than once or twice. Both knew the same earth and sky in an identical way, the same sun and moon, the same plants and animals which fed and kept the people going. Cody recognized himself in the pictures the old man made and in the way the old man picked over the language to show the meaning of his own survival. The same pictures and speech were inside Cody too. The old man's steadiness in his posture, hindsight, and ability to see into the future made Cody look up, peer more closely at their shared surroundings, and at himself too.

The second speaker exhausted his supply of words and his body deflated and folded in on itself, but his prayer and speech had their own force, hovering over everyone the remainder of night. His words were orderly and his thoughts were long ropes because his winters were full of remembered stories and advice from his old folks. So he said. Cody heard that old man's prayer years afterward, sometimes faint and sometimes close, loose on the mountain, and in the wind, still circling on.

In the old man's eyes Cody saw how ancient the elder really was, the perfect drifts of snow there, sifting down and sweeping away. In his eye sockets was also the glinting reflection at the center of everything which brought all of them through the longest and coldest nights they'd ever known, and that old man simply reminded all of them of the way things are.

I didn't forget...

That night the stranger brought and showed a very plain ceremony. Medicine, fire, and water were all present though. Those few things must have been enough, because the first few followers kept it that way for a generation. His people did things more purposefully back then.

Nearly fifty winters... Here and gone...

Quanah Parker, a Comanche Indian, had lived far from Cody's land, but they said he was the one whose ceremony the stranger brought to the *Lukachukai* mountains the night Cody and Little Man were there. All, white and Indian alike, said Quanah Parker was the center of it.

"It happened this way. Farther south, in a stretch of land his people claimed, Quanah Parker became very ill. Some of his folks doubted he was going to make it. Finally, a woman healer—one knowing herbs—was brought to him. They say she wasn't of his people, or of people up here, but was from Indian people in the far south, Mexico. Willing to help, she fixed this herb for him. Because of his recovery, Quanah Parker began to use it in a ceremony... But there's more to it, other stories..." the stranger added.

"I'm not one of Quanah Parker's group. Other tribes brought this story and his ceremony to my people. Many use it because it's good," the stranger emphasized. "I'm Cheyenne and my people are different from Comanches."

Quanah Parker was why some of Cody's relatives walked away, too. One or two spoke for the rest. "It's not meant for *us*," one man said angrily. "Comanches are old enemies. It's wrong to take a ceremony from old enemies!" Alert, Cody noted that the same relative speaking up that way was beginning to practice ceremonies of the whites.

He heard how Quanah Parker's ceremony traveled to others before it made its way to his people. Some groups shoved it away and others opened their arms. Back east and in the mid-west, a few whites who knew of it also began to disagree with Indians about it.

"Caution!" his people advised. "White leaders don't like it!"

They were cursing it and all the followers...

Elmer Stanley, a close relative, was first to warn Cody. He had soft fleshy hands and body, making him an unusual man among the family. His and Cody's paths met from time to time. On one occasion, Elmer leaned against the *hogan* wall, watching Cody sift colored sand through his fingers onto the ground. Everyone had been talking of new things among the people and their talk turned to medicine. Cody expressed mild curiosity.

Elmer leaned over, grinned broadly, and asked, "You want to go over there, too? To those crazy ones using that herb?"

He glanced sideways at Elmer's mocking tone but didn't answer as he outlined a remarkable figure in finely ground black sand. Then he rubbed dark smudges from his fingertips.

Elmer wasn't one to go away or be ignored. Chuckling, he confessed, "I went a few times." He said it slyly, with open amusement.

Cody turned away, going back to work.

"I know what they do. First time—I was really scared. Before I went I heard I was going to be sick. I heard people using medicine practice wife swapping too. I wanted to see if it was true." He laughed loudly, his open mouth showing a missing tooth, but then he became serious. "I went to find out. Afterward, I kind of lost my mind. Some say it does that... But I kept going back. Finally I went crazy. I ended up leaving my woman and children. I even got drunk. All because of that herb... That's what made me do it. Before that—well, I was a good man."

Elmer was never with a woman or children. He didn't work enough either; he drifted, though he had a lot of land and his own *hogan*. Cody watched *ye'ii* figures move from his fingers to the ground in orderly rows and didn't reply. When he didn't respond, Elmer yawned, stretching out along the wall.

He was right about one thing... Some always doubt...

Sitting on the ground with the Cheyenne and the handful of other people there that first night, Cody couldn't help but take a hard look at himself, his own life, and that of his people. The prayers of the two old men—and Elmer's words—clashed and did battle.

Compared to others there, he was nimble, young, and strong. In his mid-twenties then, he had long legs and a narrow waist. The small group called him "son," "grandson," "nephew," and by other family names though none of them except Little Man had ever met him before.

Looking back, I was the youngest there... The horse I rode up there was time itself...

New things lay before him and his people. It was hard to tell if they brought better lives or not.

Medicine was part of the new. The ceremony using it was unfamiliar, but some parts of it were centuries old.

Daily, relatives had hardships and conflicts, two kinds of suffering always among them. Yet most of the same grieving and wrathful people ended their daily stories by adding, "Peace is always in the plan of the Holy People!"

He sighed deeply, passing staff and gourd to the next person when those items came to him because he didn't have any songs yet.

At midnight the stranger told more about himself through the interpreter, painting a picture of his land and home in Oklahoma. "I traveled from there to here—with good thought, with good intention. I carry a wonderful story."

At first light, he told it, after the drum went around the *hogan* a few times and the people there had a chance to go outside and stretch.

"Some winters past, a lone woman was lost in hot dry land. She was at the mercy of the elements. Grief and loneliness overcame her because she didn't know that place at all. By and by, her life was threatened. Without water and nourishment, she knew she couldn't go on. Her people were far away and she didn't know how to return to them. Without family, and separated from her own land, it looked like she would perish out there."

The stranger paused to wipe his face with a white handkerchief, brilliant against his dark skin. "Something happened then, something good. She found this." He pointed at the altar before him.

"They say this herb spoke to her, telling her what to do and how to live. In a mysterious and holy way our people know this ground to be, it showed a way for her to survive and be reverent toward it. She listened and gathered some of these plants and packed them back to her camp. They say this herb took her home. It was wonderful what happened."

After sunrise the stranger put away his staff and other items. In closing, he said, "My relatives, all night we sat meditating. We talked to this herb and to forces in earth and the land above. We have to keep at it. It's not by chance we're here. Our old folks taught us to be devoted to certain things, to keep life coming, not only ours but everything here with us. We're all related. To this day, we're still at it. We want that same outcome, against any odds. That's why we pray for each other, pray for the ground, grass, water, pray for everything...

"We made it this far. We lived this long, through sad and lean times and we're in for more. Hard times always come around."

Everyone went outside. The stranger visited each person out there, sometimes listening quietly, sometimes hunching over to laugh deep in his chest. He was taller than everyone else. Cody finally shook his hand. Clouds of breath hung in the cold air between them—small blue fogs—before they disappeared. When the sun climbed a little higher in the sky, a hot coffee pot, burned black, appeared out of nowhere and Cody drank from a steaming enamel cup.

That's where it started...

Tired but awake, he squatted down on a sawed off log. He took off his hat, placed it beside him, and rubbed his eyes. The moist, cold forest flittered with sound and motion at one side while the sun heated his body and warmed his face.

At his *hogan* he would have been letting goats and sheep out of the corral with the rousing dogs. Care of livestock was always his work. All his training led him to that, to live as his grandparents had.

Slaps of cold wind went through his clothes and ruffled his hair. He turned away from that frosty touch and saw the horses turn too, simultaneously, in the corral.

I planned to ride to all the places my grandparents had gone... To live as my grandparents had in a new time...

He stood, stretched, and looked far north, where cold and ice lived, and stayed like that for an eternity, staring off, figuring and measuring out things, before Little Man called.

When he left that day he knew for himself what the new ceremony was. Others would say what they wanted, but he was his own man, however young.

⇅

Little did Cody know at his first participation in the new ceremony that he would become "roadman." One who conducted the new ritual, one of the first in his land. It didn't matter to him that *Washingdoon* planned to outlaw the ritual and herb for a brief time. It didn't matter that some didn't agree medicine and its ceremony were holy.

His relatives watched, waiting to see what would come of his decision to pick up the new ceremony.

Everything was already in motion, turning, when I rode up the mountain with Little Man...

In forty-six years, he came to know every part of the ceremony. Forty-six years and he was certain more knowledge was still to come from it.

During that time, he learned to be tough and direct, earning a stern reputation about the ceremony in his care and about expecting self-discipline and devotion in its followers. At an age past seventy winters, those stories always went before him.

I've been tested... My own people and Washingdoon tested me...

A grandfather and great grandfather several times over, he could still be gruff, a serious man—whether he herded livestock, or was in charge of a tipi or *hogan* full of relatives or strangers. Inside him was an old bull strangers approached cautiously. Under bushy brows Cody watched them circle him; all knew the old bull would still charge if teased a little.

He took on everyone. He never apologized when he said, "NO!" He looked younger and bigger men straight in the eye, telling them bluntly, "Don't mix this herb and altar with anything that doesn't go here! Don't mix it with alcohol!"

His eyes were hot sizzling embers and he seemed to snort out smoke when he spoke hard like that. Young people shied away from him then and his kind of straight talk.

Others backed away from the force of his words and his unapologetic glare. Those who didn't want to hear it took off right away and didn't come back, or they got angry.

It's always like that...

Otherwise, Cody lived like his neighbors and relatives; his life was steady and calm, herding sheep and goats on weekdays and doing ceremonies on weekends. He spent hot days on the mountain and cool ones on the desert. The elements seasoned him. By then his face was mapped with light crinkles and his hair had thinned. He still had the barrel chest his thin body grew into in his thirties and was still agile from herding sheep. All in all he was fit and strong. Conducting the ceremony always required it of him.

When he picked it up, its followers were very few and roadmen among his people were counted on one hand. This many years later, there were perhaps a few hundred roadmen and followers had increased many-fold.

Yes, I arrive at old age...

He was an old timer, and old timers were different from new and younger followers. Old timers weren't fast and fancy like the newcomers; they proceeded more slowly, but they were solid, through and through. When old timers talked about their early days when others moved to outlaw the ceremony, a faraway look crept over their faces and they seemed to know something the rest of them didn't. Younger generations didn't appear to notice any difference between themselves and old timers, except the obvious.

People called on him for help nearly weekly, sometimes daily, even knowing his feisty words and high expectations of them.

That was why he wasn't surprised when one golden autumn day another old timer visited one more time.

Cody had been circling his corral, like the old bull he felt inside, doing his chores and counting seasons there, and the people and relatives passing in and out of his life, when a truck door slammed near the house. In front of him his visitor was coming toward him with the precarious gait of an old dog. He couldn't help but grin as surging memories turned to affection inside him.

Cody met his guest halfway and he pulled up two metal chairs; he leaned back on his and slowly exhaled, noting infinite forces meet around him.

Loose roving clouds... Arrows of pure slanting light...

Chee

THESE DAYS HIS thoughts were bolts of lightning; they traveled that fast, indifferent to his labored baby steps. His fragile body pulled back and stalled as if it belonged to another person instead of him, while his racing mind leaped forward to its most rapid understanding. That insight flared and left. He laughed faintly at his predicament.

All the trips to Cody through snows and warmer seasons were rushing at him, competing for attention and merging together. He sorted them, and saw in that probing, a seed and ties to today's events as he pictured the short ride over there a few days before.

Curtis and me bouncing in the truck... Landscape whizzing by... A hogan collapsing inward... New pinion trees pushing up... Wide stretches of pink sand dipping and swirling in mounds under the truck... Sheep nibbling at the road... Dust noisily spraying the windshield... Wooly white clouds running place to place without giving water... A new house frame slowly standing up, boxy, modern, and small... Power lines swinging in the west, bouncing and whipping in higher wind... Survey crews in yellow stripes on both sides of the new road, their mouths moving, but their words unheard...

Resting an elbow on the door, he watched scenes zoom past where Curtis drove. Travelers on foot were not present everyday anymore. A rider on horseback still trotted over the hills though, horse and rider sharing a steady rhythm as they loped through unfenced space and faded into sagebrush hills, ever present shiny crows announcing them from atop leaning fence posts. Wagon wheel ruts still scarred the ground after countless seasons, deep enough to reroute those old wagon trails for automobiles, if passersby looked close enough. Squeaky axles and planks of lumber—rolling roughly through mud, sand and puddles seeping into thirsty dunes in a morning or two were completely gone, along with spirited mules and horses tossing their manes at bulky loads they pulled.

What he saw and didn't see made him reconsider his own beginnings and he was preoccupied with that as they rode along. His conclusion was the same today as then.

My whole life is this road… Unbroken seasons, new generations…

Yes, he was planted here as much as rows of corn were put in a field.

Born around 1900, a day's walk from where Curtis so effortlessly sped along, Chee hadn't roamed very much, or strayed too far from his birth spot in his lifetime. Without saying it, his mother and father invited him to grow roots there and he responded favorably. His mother was in her twenties then and his father twice that. His first memory might well have been of their *hogan*, a falling ring of uneven red stones in a shallow canyon not too distant, a postcard panorama from the truck window.

I wanted to pause near there but we hurried on…

A soft warm lamb forced a laugh from him when he was a few weeks old; its small bony white face nuzzled him until he reacted in an energetic burst of kicks and sounds. Of course he didn't remember those first days or the presence of his mother when he and the lamb met each other; she told him when he was older.

Her voice was a stir of pinion boughs swaying in choppy wind. "That's what happened," she said preparing a meal. Listening to her lively little story twelve winters later, Chee let loose a broad smile in spite of himself, one side of his face lifting; his eyes shining obsidian light in pale winter sun and his boyish features warming to her story.

His mother's skin was smooth and taut, her body limber, strong. Soft narrow shoulders shook with gales of laughter and her dark hair glinted red.

A brief glimpse of her floated to him even as he closed his eyes that day with Curtis. She was walking down the very same wagon road they passed, with a youthful tireless bounce—followed by a couple of toddlers, before coughing new automobiles overcame the old wagon trail to find the people hidden back here in boulders and deep sand.

Curtis had turned on the radio and its unexpected blare jolted him, interrupting his thoughts.

The past broke apart... Like glass shattering...

Instead of youth, Chee's father possessed a deep assurance his son found in the solidity of the surrounding red sandstone mesas—regal in the distance of their *hogan*. In a crisis—Chee recalled a few—his father took a stance like that, away from the center of the storm, before entering into it. But the unexpected was to come about, and with accumulating snows, his father's veil of stability began to slip, revealing him as something of a clown the older he became, accidentally, and effortlessly sliding off horses or forgetting his mother and other members of the family when he took them to town or on other trips. He put on a surprised expression then, slapping his forehead when he forgot those kinds of things. Chee folded his arms, watched, and grinned at the unexpected twist of fate.

Looking back I see the attention I received as a toddler... It was in baby talk womenfolk eagerly gave...

Thriving especially on that, he went forward, gaining strength, seasons. When he was about seven, his mother firmly pushed him toward his father and let go.

His father's care was different, consisting of a hard grip and a head-on stare always there as Chee matured. His father's pitch black eyes under thick silver brows were probing when they met Chee's, touching the core of him. He motioned Chee to follow him to the corral, into the field, into the desert, and over mountain trails. When Chee didn't keep pace, his father paused until Chee joined him. "This way," he indicated, pointing his chin in the chosen direction, leading the way.

At Curtis's age, my world was different... I witnessed it when Curtis sang in English with the radio...

Looking over his shoulder this morning, long streams of light filtered through wispy clouds. His lineages were there. Sunbeams.

Aside from his mother and father, and extended family, his teachers were earth, sky, and seasons, forces not held back or in his grasp the way he was able to hold and influence others close to him. About the world, his family kept their part simple. His parents were rarely talkers; answers about life came in other ways.

Very early, his mother put seeds in his hands and led him to a small clearing. "Right here," she said. "Put them down.'"

He dropped them recklessly into little mounds. She watched him briefly. Her own planting called. By the time he finished, he was the same muted color of the ground, indistinguishable from it. Dust coated his face, his lips, his eyelashes and hair.

His parents were specks on the other side of the field. Their voices couldn't even be heard. He went to a spot just inside the fence to play and he watched them labor over there, tiny figures under massive turning clouds in an uncleared parcel of land. He fell asleep in the field on a dusty bed, his face and arms streaked with the field's grayness, a trickling sound of irrigation water perhaps only in his imagination. For many seasons thereafter he watched earth and sky meet out there and he reflected upon their work together, their power. In old age, he still napped there when he could in warm weather, watching clouds roll overhead and the field respond to those swirls and glides.

Later, he received a small stubborn goat which taught him a thing or two about the world and himself. An eternity passed gazing into its slanted slate colored eyes, and combing its long silky wool with his rough fingers until he and the goat smelled alike. The goat returned the same fascination with Chee, waiting for him at the corral, calling out to him and nudging him forward. Chee spent long dreamy days straddled on the fence watching the goat or following it around. When he wasn't following it, it followed him.

Endless days and seasons… That's what was there…

Reaching adolescence, the unbroken stretches of seasons he knew earlier began to alter.

His family rose before dawn and didn't stop work in the field or corral until his father said, "Stop. Rest." He trailed after his father with mixed emotions about long working days but their hardness disciplined him. Work was daily practice every day of their lives, day in, day out.

He observed parenting from the beginning, too. Parenting models were everywhere, in the wild, as well as among people.

To his surprise, about that time, almost entirely through observation, it suddenly struck him that the relationship between his father and mother, which had survived seasons, had also been strained and that there were times when it truly could have gone either way. Innocence about his parents' devotion to one another he'd held as a younger man slowly started to crumble, but they were always thoughtful parents. Chee was puzzled over those two seemingly opposing truths for a while.

In the same way, human character showed itself to him early on. Sometimes he tried to close his eyes to it. Nevertheless the sting of jealousy, the burn of hatred, anger, frustration, and the numbness of despair, along with the warmth of tenderness, encouragement, and kindness were always a part of the people, his family and strangers. Everywhere he went raw emotions rose, sometimes running wild. Hurtful words were aimed at each other; accusations about possessions and family relationships, among other things, were daily events. Sometimes someone left in that heat never to return.

Life is joyful and tragic... All of it must be noted... Shared...

Chee saw his father stop what he was doing to listen briefly to hot exchanges nearby and turn to see who spoke before going back to his work. He didn't advise Chee on those incidents when his young son turned to him. Chee just remembered his father's black eyes directly upon him, waiting.

Raw emotions are inside me, too... Frustration... Anger... Sadness... Fear... They're inside everyone...

He argued with his brothers playfully and more seriously as they grew older together. Differences worked themselves out and most of the family stayed close over time.

That outcome was not always clear or certain for everybody. He witnessed families split when emotion ruled. Conflict existed among and with his extended family and his parents bore the brunt of it, too.

One day an unrestrained and wildly beautiful young woman dressed in a full dark blue skirt marched to their field and began to scream at the three of them. "This is mine! You took it without my agreement! Leave!" Her words, abrupt as her presence and her claim to the field, startled Chee. She glared at him and he felt a searing burn. As the young woman turned toward his father and quickly toward his mother, back and forth, her blue skirt flapped happy little whirls, at odds with her red hot rage.

His mother and father were taken by surprise. Their uncertain response was silence as their accuser paced under a giant rustling cottonwood casting cool and serene shadows on all of them. She wanted immediate action, elevating her shoulders, ready to pounce. His mother and father stood their ground, gazing at each other.

Finally, his mother said softly and firmly, "No," meeting the eyes of the young woman. Then his mother turned away.

Chee observed everything. All three of them were leery of each other. He saw a kind of dance.

The young woman leaped in a quick twirl and jumped on his mother's back who was stunned by the speed of it.

"Don't say that to me," the other woman screamed, pulling and shaking his mother. "You must return what is mine! Give it back!"

Chee's father rushed in from behind her and grabbed the young woman's flinging arms, saying, "Whoa! Whoa!" He held her tightly but she kicked and hurled her legs. Her skirt flapped and snapped this way and that.

Chee's father pointed her to the gate and then released her. She dashed away, but not before she stopped and threatened, "What you want will never be! I will see to it." In that instant, her face was stormy, ancient. Her hair had come loose and long strands whirled around her face.

Feuds and turmoil exist generation to generation...

In his teens when Chee witnessed the incident, he was of medium height and very slender, with his father's blue-black hair and glassy black eyes. He ate well enough, with one or two exceptions when his family became especially frugal. Later, at seventeen, his extended family took inquisitive second glances at him and strangers expressed interest in him as well. Chee ignored everyone and went back and forth between the family's field and livestock, until the afternoon his father met him at the corral.

"Visitors are here," his father said casually, leaning back against the corral post. The sheep meandered, chewing brush behind Chee.

"Your relatives are suggesting women... Marriage..." His father's eyes were thoughtful, as he, too, chewed a long smooth green stem. "Marriage for you."

He masked surprise. Looking eye to eye with his father, he didn't know it then but he was seeing himself, and his future.

It was like the day with Curtis... In the side mirror everything behind me fell away... Then ahead many things flew at us...

They penned sheep. His father walked unhurriedly back to the *hogan*.

Chee didn't go there; saddling his horse, he rode off for a while toward the red mesas.

"Marriage!" he whispered.

A growling stomach soon brought him back and his mother made bread for him; marriage was not mentioned again for a while.

On the day it came, Chee was a day or two past eighteen. His small family took charge, handling the whole affair. That was not a simple matter because two or three often did not see eye to eye. Eventually, after a couple of get-togethers and after all of them had fully expressed themselves, the family settled it.

"It's done," an uncle said with a twinkle in his eye and those who had disagreed earlier were now friendly and satisfied.

Up to that day, Chee stayed in the background making few comments either for or against family plans. By then, impending marriage held no alarm; the short delay discussing it had made that much difference.

Seasons work incomprehensibly... One day the dark sky is full of raging storms and the next is so quiet, bright and clear...

They suggested a young girl who had never been married, someone unlike anyone he knew, and she changed his world.

There are points in life where everything turns on a single decision or choice to be made...

For him, the most significant was that day he and Susie made their agreement with each other.

"She's pleasant," her family said earlier.

"Industrious," they added.

The day he finally met her, he was quietly pleased with the turn of events and he pondered the fortune coming his way. He forgot about the others around him as he eyed this stranger, his bride. It was necessary to be discreet though because he was taught that way. Still, he found it difficult keeping his eyes away.

Sitting beside her, he feigned indifference. Suddenly she glanced at him, into his eyes. Hers were the brown color of pinions, with long thin lashes resembling black spider legs. The sun stopped moving. Everything stopped. Just the warm brown irises moved. He wondered if she thought much of him, hoping for the best.

For a few weeks afterward, he suspected that "yes" and "no" might be the only words she ever spoke. Thin and tall as his shoulder, he approached her as if she might break.

At the beginning, starting out their life together, the two of them had little cash; they traded livestock, crops, and other goods for their staples and other necessities. Chee cleared surrounding sagebrush and trees to plant a patch of melons and corn for them, upon the advice of his father. Most of the labor he did alone. In the springtime, he planted, and the rest of the year, he cared for a few livestock belonging either to Susie's or his family. It was about 1920.

Since the day they met, Susie was always near. In their life together, their periods of separation were only for a few days at a time. She proved to be much stronger than the fragile girl he first thought she might be. She went without many things more prosperous women had and she always toiled over her children. In summer and winter, her face burned from working alongside him in the field, in the desert, and corral. Her days were full of those tasks. At night she made clothes by hand for all the family as did most every woman at the time.

Separate little tasks of life all strung together...

One time their wagon became mired in a rare heavy rainstorm right near where Curtis and he approached this homestead. That time, Susie, with the children, helped free the wagon again. He could still see those glistening faces in splashing rain and their hair hanging in soggy strands down their foreheads while water ran in rivulets under their feet and became a network of tiny rushing streams, turning the earth into mush under them.

His and Susie's wagon rides were now put away. Yet those fragrant evenings, full of sounds from earth and sky and fiery falling suns he witnessed on horseback and from squeaking wagon beds were stored inside him creating rich vivid dreams, soft and deep, that made him want to linger in sleep.

Nearly sixty winters gone... Yet here I am with the same girl my family chose way back then... Our lives going from wagons to trucks...

When Curtis parked in front of the house after returning from Cody's, in the window was Susie. She was always looking out for him, a habit she started decades before. He went inside to tell her what had come of his visit with Cody.

Today, he looked at their house critically, built about twenty five years before with the help of Hunter. Studying the addition to it, done after fifteen years, it was strong and secure.

Then, the tipi ground beckoned. He stood and slowly wobbled over to it, recalling his words to Cody.

"One of my children falters right now. He needs help. His mind wanders. He says he can't go on anymore.

"It's Dusty."

His voice was matter of fact with little emotion; to him it sounded distant, a pebble skimming a rocky surface, yet louder than expected, with a bit of echo.

Cody rubbed tiny creases on his forehead but didn't say much. It was his presence that comforted.

The two of them sat together for a while afterward, watching day slip past and he saw and felt the steadiness in its movement. The same steadiness was in Cody and in himself, too, pulsing in his veins and in his measured breaths.

We go way back together...

Susie

THE INNOCENT GIRL-BRIDE of half a century earlier peered out the east window. She leaned against an arm of a heavily padded upholstered chair, watching the man she'd known since she was fifteen years old. He walked slowly away from the house, pulling a wooden chair, its legs scraping hard ground. Her own limbs were heavy as she pressed back on the chair.

We weren't always like this...

Just before the first light snow of the season they met. Two of his uncles came to her family. One announced, "It's time my son finds a mate." All her family leaned forward to hear what he was going to say next. That's what she was told.

"Three sheep," was their first offer. One of her family members suggested hopefully, "Perhaps some other goods as well?" It was a modest sum for the day and for who they all were.

Chee's family nodded when their discussion reached that closing point. They were far from wealthy and hers was no richer. The necessary bartering eventually satisfied everyone. It was simply a detail in a larger picture.

In exchange, Susie honored the agreement between two families, and took her place beside Chee in the *hogan*.

I was too shy but I was curious... A new part of life was coming...

Her family, protective because of her size, age, and innocence, met his eyes that day and held him in a tight vise, "Treat her well," they warned. She watched the exchange between the two sides, but didn't say much.

"She's young."

"She's dear to us."

Quietly, but firmly, they advised about life and her and her young man's duty to future children. One speaker, bolder than others, hinted at more private matters. Tilting her head toward one shoulder the brazen woman said loudly, "Some people aren't satisfied with their mates and go elsewhere for company."

I looked down at the ground... I was alone... That woman, an aunt of mine, frightened and shamed me...

The aunt added sharply, as if what she already said wasn't enough, "Don't be lazy either! We didn't say you were like that!" She looked directly at Susie and Susie felt humiliated. The aunt was hefty and her booming voice made Susie flinch. Nothing about the aunt was soft.

Chee told Susie sometime later, "I want to stay away from her!" Susie smiled brightly because of his observation and comment.

Almost everyone gave advice... Finally, Chee and I were alone in the small hogan at my family's place...

Such a long time ago! She saw frozen ground and thawing of trees.

Still at the window, her gaze went southward. Fall had circled around again; daylight already transformed, becoming softer. Then her eyes settled again on the man sitting outside, looking toward the tipi ground.

More than sixty winters ago we were strangers...

Immediately after their marriage, it was clear to her that Chee was what his and her families claimed. Though not at all worldly in the matter of choosing a mate for herself, she had relied on their judgment, and what she witnessed later seemed to bear out their claims.

At the time, in appearance, he was of medium height with long blue-black hair and glassy obsidian eyes. He was lean and spry. He seemed to be well taught and disciplined, showing care about himself and others. His warmth was apparent from the start.

Those qualities didn't make it any easier for me to be alone with him the first time... We were strangers...

Vagueness flitted across her face but a pin of light shone in her dark eyes. The marriage night, they looked at each other from different sides of the *hogan* and made separate beds, silently reflecting upon the day's events, and advice given. She slept soundly and forgot she had a mate when she awoke the next morning. Then she heard him moving about and she put a hand over her mouth to muffle surprise.

Now she laughed. Her laughter was whispery and in it was the girl-bride she'd been seasons past.

When she got up that morning, her hair came loose and carelessly hung well below her hips. Chee sat like a boulder in front of her, staring openly; he seemed unable to move. They met each other's eyes but that was all. The *hogan* was so still, frozen in the look passing between them, except for sounds of fire flicking in the stove and wind spitting through the smoke hole.

Their first days together were quiet and awkward. For answers, beside "yes" and "no," she gave Chee a wide-eyed, head-on gaze and a tilted chin. She often caught him watching her and her face became hot and red, and she quickly fled out the door.

Inexperienced at cooking then, she did what she could, and Chee accepted what she offered.

He spent most of his time taking care of my family's live-stock... He wanted to help when I tried household chores I didn't know...

She ignored his offers. Then he seemed to decide that she was best left alone. Meanwhile, the men in the family waited for him outside, taunting him about being a newly-wed, in fragmented English of their day.

Too bashful to really face Chee and talk to him yet, little by little, she felt more secure in his presence each passing day. Then came the morning he approached her. He slowly put his hand over hers and deftly moved it up her arm to eventually rest on her face, cupping her chin in his hand. He was a bit clumsy, laughing softly as if he saw that clumsiness in himself too. Then they studied each other's faces. His eyes were black pools. Deep. Deep. Placing his other arm around her small waist, he nudged her to him. She permitted the embrace but pushed back as if caught in indecision. His body was so warm, comforting and inviting. To her own surprise, she returned his embrace in a strong reach for him.

After that stirring morning, she accepted his presence completely. Then she showed him that she really did know how to talk, astonishing him with how much she had to say, his eyes shining with humor. Usually though she was reserved, preferring solitude and observation before letting her inquisitive and curious nature show.

We've matured together through peace and storms... This world and seasons challenged us...

Almost three years later, their first child was born at summer sheep camp. She was nearly eighteen. Her mother caught the newborn in a net of tender names

"My baby! My baby!"

The infant showed strong lungs and limbs right off, responding to his maternal grandmother with a wail and he attempted swift little kicks. Then he tried both his arms and legs, boxing and kicking anyone who cradled him, until she laced him onto a sturdy cradleboard, and that was his place for his first few weeks. That's how Hunter met the world.

Chee wasn't around; he worked in his own family's field. Anyway, there was still the old etiquette about seeing a mother-in-law face-to-face. Both he and Susie's mother tried to respect it. Nevertheless, Chee and Susie lived at her family's home site, where he and her mother tactfully stayed out of each other's way. Blunders occurred though.

Once, at a large gathering, Susie's mother and another woman had to unfold a piece of canvas and hold it up for Susie's mother to stand behind because of his presence. Everyone saw the two women lift it in a very determined fashion, quickly shaking it out. It made a whooshing sound and then the canvas darted past. The other woman was heftier than Susie's mother and to see her dash by made everyone gleeful. Even Susie's mother laughed when she caught her breath.

Susie and Chee later enjoyed those incidents again and again when nights were long and ice covered the ground, as did so many others who were there.

At her first child birthing, Chee was glad she had her mother there, in place of him. And in those days, rules were different.

He told her, "That worked better for you. Your mother was there to comfort you and to see that it went safely. I wouldn't have known what to do."

He was right... I always leaned on my mother and grandmother... Their experience was more stable than my own shifting emotions...

Chee worked relentlessly for her family, herding sheep, chopping wood and transporting water by wagon. He rose at dawn to begin his tasks and he stayed busy until evening. He also helped his own relatives with labor and goods, when he could. Distance prevented too many visits, along with a lack of his own wagon, but it was during one of those times when the two of them went visiting that Chee's own mother asked, "When's the baby due?"

"What?" Chee asked in surprise.

It was too early to show her second pregnancy but Chee's mother knew it first.

I haven't thought very much about how to live... I know how life goes only by watching it... Only by watching others... Only by completing my work...

The second child was born about two years after the first. They called her Mary. Unlike Hunter, she was frail and delicate with a weak cry and a tiny appetite. Her skin turned sallow right away. Then Susie's breasts became heavy and swollen because the baby wouldn't nurse. Alarmed, she took the infant to her mother, Hunter trailing.

"She won't nurse."

"Are you hungry, baby?" her mother asked, opening her arms wide. Susie handed over the baby and plopped onto a chair, relieved that her mother had answers. That was when a special attachment started to form between Mary and her maternal grandmother, who later often whisked Mary away for short times.

In a while the baby livened up. Mary began to suckle Susie's finger, then a nipple. The child's natural skin color returned.

For several months, their family thrived. Then Susie grew thinner and became pale again. Her skin sunk beneath her eyes. In that way the third child presented itself. Overall in good health and in good spirit, Susie's small frame puffed out as she performed all her motherly duties and helped herd her family's sheep. It was then autumn and the weather was just right.

Each day she brought the sheep in from grazing about midday, when the sun reached a certain place. Hunter sometimes kept her company when she didn't go too far. Full of energy, he always discovered something to occupy his attention. He was almost six then. Chee met her at the sheep corral to help open the gate and secure the corral.

On one of those days after taking out the sheep, she delivered her third child. Chee was repairing the horse corral, lifting his eyes now and then to scan the horizon where she promised to stay that day. Mary was away with her grandmother. When Chee heard sheep bells, he started walking towards the corral. Susie met him but didn't stop, rushing past and hurrying toward the house. Hunter followed, whining, "I'm hungry. I'm hungry."

A little while later, Hunter went racing to Chee, as he closed the corral.

"Baby," he yelled. "Baby..."

"What?"

"Baby..." He pointed at the house, excitedly. Chee picked up his pace and headed over. He flung the door wide open and there lay Susie crosswise on the bed, trying to wrap a wet newborn in a towel. It was a red, blotchy-skinned boy with no hair. Chee looked at the tiny figure resembling a miniature old man and greeted him with a husky laugh. "So we meet!" he said. He looked into Susie's eyes and nodded.

She was sweaty and tired, too exhausted to speak at the hurried event. Hunter came back inside, just in time to hear his brother's first little squeal.

I and Chee have taken chances in our lives, but they were necessary... He might think differently about it... After all our days together, we are still different people...

By the time Sammie arrived, Hunter resembled his mother in appearance and in other ways as well. Everyone noticed the similar facial features and the slight build. Like her in an earlier time, he never said much either, but "yes" and "no," until he became really interested in the matter at hand. That's what happened when he first saw Sammie.

He started talking to him immediately, climbing on the bed to lie down beside him.

"Hey, baby, what you doing?"

Sammie stopped moving and lay perfectly still, as if he really heard. Chee pulled Hunter down after he accidentally kicked her.

The fourth child was a tiny replica of Chee and he entered the world quietly. There were no surprises with his birth. Chee named him Wayne.

Sammie just turned four and always acted as Wayne's protector. By then Sammie had grown a head full of shiny black hair which his mother cut only once between then and the day he was born.

Childbearing is now behind me.... Life's quiet... My children have been on their own for a long time... As it should be... As it should be...

Wayne walked at eleven months. He fell all the time, accompanied by a thud and tears the size of large raindrops.

Sammie was always there to yank him up and clumsily wipe teardrops across Wayne's face. Because Wayne didn't stay on his feet for very long, he was usually covered with bruises on his face and arms. He always looked as if his tears had just ended. His eyes stayed red and his face had permanent stains from teardrops. He had the same squeal Sammie had, but with more volume. When Hunter or Mary teased him, no one was spared his ear-splitting shrieks.

Austin arrived next, when Susie was in her late twenties, or was it her early thirties?

I don't count seasons the same way as my children...

It happened one memorable night traveling to Chee's family who then lived about thirty miles away, six canyons distant. They made an overnight ride in the wagon, traveling most of the way without meeting anyone. Only crows saw the wagon and cawed at it from above while an occasional jackrabbit jumped clear of whirling wheels.

As evening stars sprinkled overhead, Chee yanked the reins tight and yelled, "Whoa! Whoa!" The children echoed him, "Whoa! Whoa!" While he unhitched the horses, Susie emptied the wagon bed.

"Help start a fire. Eat and then sleep," Chee told the children.

Hunter and Mary gathered kindling and before they knew it, Chee had a bright fire blazing.

Blue night gleamed; landscape was as clear as day. The early night turned cold quickly. Susie made hot drinks with bread. That was enough though. In those days, their meager meals were always enough.

All of them forgot about the cold when Chee spoke.

"It happened here. This is where everything happened."

The children climbed into the wagon bed after Chee

made the fire roar and they hushed. They all lay in the wagon, packed tightly together on sheepskins, looking at the sky. "Enemy warriors used to raid here."

"Who did they raid?" Mary asked.

"Us."

"We weren't here," Mary said.

"Oh, yes, we were."

Chee told about raids. He described the raiders.

"They didn't look dangerous, but they were capable of doing us great harm."

"Quivers hung down their backs, and the warriors were thin and strong."

The children said they were able to see them.

"Their language sounded different from ours."

The children seemed to be trying to imagine another language.

After Chee finished his storytelling, he got up and lay near the fire on the ground. He woke Hunter and had him move to the fire, too. Susie snuggled more deeply into her bed of sheepskins. Beside her lay Mary.

Nothing is secret about the life process but who can explain it? One by one, my children came forth... From seasonal cycles... Lines of people... Families gathering and leaving...

After a while, she woke with a sharp twinge in her lower back. Around camp, earth glowed, pulsating in blue light. Fire danced and spit out pieces of wood. A shooting star came down just above the wagon. She sat up and covered Mary and Wayne more snugly. Chee and Hunter curled on their sides near the fire.

She climbed off the wagon, making it squeak a little as she moved, and she dug out more blankets from under the wagon seat. She threw them down on the ground beside the fire. Then, she lay down right there to bring Austin into the world.

Chee heard and sat up.

Not too much time elapsed before Austin softly touched down on a store bought blanket, in much the same way the star earlier came to earth.

He lay quietly sucking a tiny fist while fire danced at his side.

Chee poured warm water into the only pan they had with them and quickly washed Austin with a warm cloth. Then he gave the pan to Susie.

The other children slept soundly.

Chee wrapped Austin in a dish towel and tucked him in the crook of her arm. Her soft body and warm breath kept him safe the rest of the night.

Seasons don't pause for any one, and in that wheel, we see how life is laid down...

The cold was uncommon so early in the year. Chee kept the fire burning brightly the rest of the night and was up at the crack of dawn as always each day of his life. He didn't wake her after her restless night. She was a bundle on the ground.

Shortly after sunrise, she opened her eyes and heard Chee moving about. She looked around for him and saw him brushing off glittery frost trimming the metal on the wagon.

The aroma of coffee was in the air.

"You can rest in the wagon. Are you too weak?"

"Help me up," she said. He looked doubtful but he took Austin from her side and helped her stand.

Slowly, she moved around the wagon bed, brushing away cold shiny flakes close to Mary, Sammie, and Wayne. Then she turned her attention to Austin.

One at a time the children rose and Chee poured coffee for them. He also set out a small meal. They drank their coffee with loud sounds of appreciation.

The children didn't notice Austin until he began to make his own sounds. Then they all had a chance to hold him. Each one inspected him, from his flat little nose to the soles of the feet.

Susie said, "It's too cold for that. Cover him."

By then the sun stood up and the family had thawed in morning light.

The agreement Chee and I try to keep goes far beyond us... Only we know what's at stake...

Chee and Hunter hitched the horses to the wagon and by mid-morning, they were on their way again. Mary cuddled Austin the rest of the way. Mary was not yet nine but a knowing babysitter after watching over both Sammie and Wayne.

As the wagon rolled out, the children's voices lingered on the trail, amidst those of the crows. Susie half sat and half lay in the wagon bed, watching Mary with Austin, and listening to her young family and wagon wheels turn.

The past is before me daily though I move steadily toward each rising sun...

The next child born to them was Dusty when Susie was definitely in her thirties. A couple more years went by before Richard was born.

They moved to a new location offering better grazing for their livestock, after Richard's birth. Chee, with Hunter's help, constructed a small wood frame house beside a large *hogan*. Hunter was a little taller than Chee then and he had really filled out. He seemed capable of eating a whole sheep by himself. Susie had become a weaver. Annually she traded hers, and her mother's, modest sized rugs to the local trader for nails, construction tools, and other supplies. She didn't weave all the time, and not during her pregnancies, but she wove between the births of her children, at her mother's urging.

On one such trip, she gave birth in one of the back rooms of the trading post. The story of that incident was repeated so many times that Chee said he had heard the story at least twice from almost everyone involved. The child delivered there came two months early.

It happened that Hunter had taken her and his grandmother to the trading post in the wagon with all the other children. They went the distance in a little less than an hour. It was on a weekend and normally the married couple from Colorado who owned the store was on hand to visit and help her and her mother, but not that time. They had left the care of the store in their son's hands. He had just returned from school in Colorado and was then about twenty-five years old. He knew the trading business, spoke the language of the people roughly, but hadn't any experience delivering children. His name was Edmond, a serious, stout young man, and he had recently married a young girl who knew nothing about Susie's people. She and Edmond met in school in Denver.

On the wagon ride to the trading post, she and her mother had a lively conversation going with all the children. Then her lower back started to cramp and she tried to ignore it. She grew quiet while the children sang and argued with each other. It was a rough ride, always a little uncomfortable. That day her body felt each bump and swerve the wagon took but she kept this to herself. By the time she climbed off, there was strong cramping in her pelvis but other than that warning, she had no reason to be alarmed since it was much too early for the baby to arrive. She was anxious to conclude business.

Life is surprising... Who can guess what will happen?

They walked into the store and a line of people were ahead of them. "Edmo!" they called the young man helping them. She didn't complain about her aching back and cramping pelvis because her mother was always overly concerned. She also knew that Hunter would turn the wagon right around and Chee really needed the nails and other supplies for a house frame he was constructing that very day. Her mother chatted with other women there and they giggled together while Susie's pain intensified. More nervous by the minute, she unconsciously made her hands into soft fists until the most painful moments passed.

By the time Edmo took Susie's mother's rugs and they had settled on a price, the youngest of the children were impatient and irritable. Susie bought some crackers and sent those out to them with Mary. She selected all her supplies and food items, and printed cotton cloth to make skirts for Mary and herself, and waited for Hunter to carry those outside. Her mother was still making purchases.

The pain became overbearing; it really was time to leave. Her lower back exploded in pain. She sucked in air and clenched her teeth. Unconsciously, she began to rub her back and when the cramps and pain subsided, she walked in circles around the store. When her mother finished her purchases, she asked where Hunter was.

"With Austin and Dusty," Susie said and let out an involuntary gasp. She was barely able to stand.

"What's wrong?" her mother asked anxiously. "Can it be that the baby wants to be born at the trading post instead of home?"

Susie nodded, "That must be it. Yes..."

She was swaying at the counter when she saw Edmo's new wife come out of the storage room. Mary steadied her, with Sammie's help.

"Edmond!" she heard his wife call. "Come here. Quickly! Quickly!"

While Edmond guided her into the stockroom, Hunter reappeared and helped settle his mother on a long row of wooden boxes. She tried very hard to be in charge but everything happened too swiftly. She wanted to tell Hunter and Mary to take the younger ones home but all she could say was, "The baby is on the way!"

Edmo and his wife scurried around her while Hunter went out of the room to watch the front of the store. The line of customers temporarily broke. All buying and trading ceased while Edmo and his wife attended her, despite her own strong protests.

She always was very modest and had never interacted with others outside of her own people; furthermore, she didn't want to be teased about delivering her baby in a trading post, with the help of a very young trader! With the help of Edmo! That was just too much! She thought it would be better to have the baby outside, any place away from there!

"I can do this alone!" she insisted, almost angrily. Edmo didn't have to explain what she said to his wife. Her disagreement was very loud and clear.

His young wife firmly but silently shook her head "no" at Susie's words. She saw the exchange between them. It made her even more resistant, but what could she do?

Outside, the livestock brought to the trading post to be sold waited patiently for Edmo's attention. Some goats grazed outside the trading post corral and a couple of hired-hands sat on the fence and laughed about the baby that brought business to a standstill while the goats bleated and wandered farther away. Hunter told her this later.

Her youngest child, Richard, recklessly climbed the posts which supported a narrow porch roof leading into the store. Hunter occasionally went out and pulled him down just before he crashed to the ground or managed to climb all the way up on the roof. Hunter bribed him with an amber sucker and all the others settled down, agreeing to wait patiently for their mother.

Susie's mother didn't like the whole situation one bit, either. She gave a stormy frown of disapproval to her and went back and forth between her and the children. Susie thought of escaping somehow! Then, when the younger children each had possession of a sucker, Richard making loud smacking sounds, her mother gave in and climbed onto a stack of full flour sacks, the only place to sit in the stock room, to help Susie give birth by offering barely audible words of encouragement. Then she, seeing that her mother accepted the awkward situation as it was, also gave in.

A few minutes later her mother and, yes, Edmo helped her coax the child into the world. She was unusually weak afterward. Edmo and his wife gave the baby a blanket from the store and immediately wrapped the newborn in it; they were flushed with excitement. The top sack of flour where Susie's mother had sat had ripped quietly open. When she climbed off the flour sacks to cuddle the infant, her dark skirts were caked with flour.

Outside, Hunter lost track of Richard and Dusty. Mary and Wayne went to find them. Hours later, when all the family were accounted for, Hunter and Edmo steered Susie outside and put her in the wagon bed—with Edmo's wife giving instructions on how best to do it. By then it was nearly evening, but they still had light as they started home.

Susie wasn't accepting of that kind of pampering; she wanted to walk alone and sit-up on the ride back but her mother, noting rings around Susie's eyes and damp skin, was extra cautious and took the side of the young traders, insisting that she lay down all the way. Hunter drove the team of horses slower than he did on the way over, and as a result it was after dark when the family arrived.

Now and then, I've been ill and weak, but no more than other women... I and Chee have always relied on guidance from elders to stay well.... On plants and herbs... Our agreement on all these matters makes our days what they are......

Chee met them half way. He had started to worry and saddled his favorite horse and had come to look for them. She was asleep with the baby in her arms but woke as soon as she heard Chee's voice. Then Hunter traded places with his father; Hunter rode the horse home.

Susie's mother melted into darkness. She did not address Chee.

The rest of the ride had a quiet hypnotic rhythm to it; there was only the sound of the creaking wagon and horses moving through early moonlight. The younger children were asleep beside Susie after their exciting afternoon, holding sticky suckers in their hands. When she crawled out of the wagon later, a sucker stuck on a strand of her hair. The baby's new blanket was sticky and dirty from the other children's welcoming caresses.

In the excitement of the event, Edmo, speaking in his rough Navajo, asked Susie what she planned on naming the child.

"Kee," Susie answered. Edmond understood that Susie said *Kee*, but Edmo's young wife wasn't familiar with her people's names. His wife told everyone that the baby's name was Keith, and she loved to tell the story of his birth to anyone who would listen. Eventually, Keith was the name on all his records.

Into the family of mostly men then came Sarah, almost two decades after Mary. She had little round glassy agate eyes and a head full of light colored hair when she was born. The presence of her delicate little body balanced the household. By then Mary had gone off on her own, as had Hunter. At first the boys weren't sure how to treat a little girl. They tried ignoring her and leaving her solely in their mother's care but Sarah's presence and her tiny figure began to grow on them. When she began to walk and talk, her bony legs and high pitched voice were so endearing that they all voluntarily alternated supervising and pampering her, allowing their mother to do other tasks around the house.

Next, Ross was born and it was Sarah's turn to play little mother. She and Ross were inseparable. All through their school years and into adult life, Sarah was Ross's intermediary.

When the last child was born, Susie named him Curtis. That was about 1946 or close to it.

Life is not without roots… Each time I gave birth I felt their hold.…

PART THREE

New Moon

Daybreak song

RECORDED BY KISH HAWKINS

Cody

ON THE NIGHT he went to that first ceremony with Little Man, his people were coming out of upheaval, a time foretold. Their eyes and talk were often full of dismay. Many clamored for better times, old times.

I wanted to live as my grandparents did but there's no going back...

On another night in meditation, he saw shadowy figures lurk on the road ahead, his path to the future. Running back and forth in an unsettling way, those black shapes were defiant and mocking.

"What are they? What are they doing?" He raked his mind.

Whatever they were, whatever they were up to, had to be faced... That's how life carries on...

His mother's brother, Wind, was the one who told Cody about that first prayer meeting and suggested he go with Little Man since he himself couldn't be there. He was also the one who showed Cody how to study things.

Wind was a chanter, a singer. His work was the most accepted and oldest among them, yet Wind attended the new ceremony as soon as it arrived.

He was harshly criticized.

"That's not for us!"

"That's not tradition!"

"That's not good!"

"He must be crazy!"

At the worst and most cutting, Wind was unfazed, stayed diligent in his daily work and traditional healing, and remained soft spoken.

"My nephew, I see a place for this in my life." Stroking his black silky mustache, he stared up at stringy white clouds running through space. That was Wind's thinking.

In the days which had arrived, Wind had seen young people and children depart for school in growing numbers. Too often they left their homes fully themselves and came back with a downward cast in their eyes. Along with that, their use of land, and thoughts about it, the earth, altered. After finishing school, many didn't wait to head to town or trade their open land for a square house, and their language for another. Homesteads and livestock were replaced by small wages. He commented on this to his nephew.

Going away sometime means leaving a part of ourselves behind... A kind of slow dying...

Wind saw things from far away, a sentinel on a hilltop. Since he was a smaller man than others, an astonishing vision was what he used to make his way through seasons. Then his limbs and energy easily shifted to meet what he saw in the distance.

Cody's life skills came from Wind and he took Cody very seriously. Under Wind's arm, Cody learned to care for livestock, and animals in the wild, and his *hogan* and family.

"Look here," he said so quietly Cody had to lean to catch all his words in early morning when they went to chop wood, and axes were flying. "Old knowledge and skills have value. If we know and live by them, we live long and don't need much. Look around, nephew, what do you see?"

A few of my relatives took new opportunities... A different kind of life sprang up on the edge of towns...

All that Wind had taught him so many seasons past had been sifting in Cody's mind when Chee arrived at his house a few days before. When Chee left, there was more to sift—recalling both families, Chee's and his own, through five decades. That led back to himself and a recent event. He had to face it. What Chee said reminded him of it, in the same way that Wind had made him look at many situations and size them up.

Before he knew it, a single tear rolled down the curve of his cheekbone. Quietly it slid from the outer corner of his eye and hung on his jaw. Then he gave out a giant sob and shuddered. Pulling out a wrinkled handkerchief and blowing his nose, that instant was gone.

Very few people imagined the old bull of a man ever had sorrow, or that he might cry like that. Yet here it was. A flaw, a weakness in him, a deep fresh wound.

Inside his house the steady beat of a water drum started under the bleating of his sheep, dingy smudges appearing and disappearing on the rise behind him. It was a high pitched drum beat; the drummer used a rapid double stroke. One of his grandsons was the drummer; they all favored the more popular fast and fancy songs which younger men sang these days, the kind grandson Quanah sang.

Cody watched three sheep nibble at nearby brush as he stood to follow them toward the corral. Another grandson was bringing them in for the day. The sheepherder was a preteen and he went into the house when he saw his grandfather coming to take over. Cody knew his herd by sight, and scanning it, knew immediately that one was missing. He'd have to go and find it. He approached the hill the sheep had come down.

In the bloom of manhood… We had a dream for you…

As a child Quanah was like a lamb Cody protected and secured from coyotes and other predators. He grew up to eventually speak his own language and English, but as a child, he used only one. When he was knee high, Cody put a gourd rattle in his right hand and showed him how to produce the pleasing rhythmic sounds in his ceremonial songs. This music was different from the older chants of the people.

Later Quanah sang and drummed with other boys his age. All of them were rough and tough, with grimy hands and faces, hardly resembling would-be musicians. First, their dirty clumsy hands learned to tie the drum. It took months to really conquer that and their combined strength was needed to lace the rope tight enough around the drum hide. It usually popped loose after the drumstick struck the hide a few times. Then, as they learned to beat the drum with firm and steady strokes, they pierced the drum hide with over-exuberance and ruined it. Cody held his tongue and produced another one.

They tried their voices next. They wanted to sing the way the men did, so rapturously with closed eyes, melodious words flying like bright birds out of the singers' mouths and hearts. The boys' first efforts were clumsy and endearing. They tried their high pitched voices and put those with the irregular drumbeats. It was a necessary learning stage. After all, they were just boys, about ten and eleven years of age.

Quanah began to go to prayer meetings held at Cody's place then. Everyone in attendance accepted all the boys' first rough attempts at singing. Quanah and the other boys sat up all night, observing all the older singers carefully.

Seasons shuffled and miracles occurred. The boys'

faces and bodies took on promising new forms. Their voices deepened and became more resonant and their drumming was confident, steady and strong. They sat on their knees for hours at a stretch and their thighs were muscular and firm. The number of songs they mastered grew and grew.

When they all sang together at the right time, everything in the world met at one starry point and became one voice — one song, one brilliant point, one insight.

Rays of light... Fluttering of birds...

About then, Cody began to teach Quanah about the crescent moon altar. He showed him where to get sand and how to build the mound just so. Next Cody encouraged Quanah to travel over the country with other roadmen on their journeys to other tribes and on pilgrimages to the sacred garden.

Quanah learned each roadman's steps, his special teachings, and inconsistencies as well. It was an invigorating period and he couldn't wait to share his experiences with Cody.

One time he returned in a somber mood. In his late teens then, he was a fine looking young man with wide shoulders and a trim waist. His brown eyes were troubled.

"Grandfather," he said. "I thought all roadmen lived by the teachings of this altar."

Cody thought of the roadman who just brought Quanah home.

Cody asked, "What do you think now?"

"Some don't."

"Yes, grandson," he nodded, "you said it."

Quanah went on, learned to be fire chief, arranging charcoal into various shapes and with those tasks, how to pray. His experience was stacking up. Finally, Cody showed Quanah how to tie tipi poles, lift them, and the white tipi grandly into the sky, and to stake it firmly down. Quanah learned it so well that he could set up a large tipi by himself with just one other man if absolutely necessary. It was hard but it could be done.

Such promise...

Cody had gone a little way searching for his missing sheep, remembering Quanah as he last saw him, sitting in the tipi on his knees and rolling tobacco. He heard Quanah's prayer begin. He saw him hold a long colorful beaded staff with a bright fan in his left hand and the gourd rattle in his right, shaking it confidently and firmly with a swish, swish, swish, his voice rising toward the smoke hole of the tipi. He saw him on his knees holding the drum with his left hand and the intricately carved drum stick in his right, tirelessly moving around the tipi until he had drummed for more than a dozen singers who sung four songs each. Quanah usually sang with them, even the women and young girls just learning.

About three years back, Quanah began to compose his own songs. Those compositions surprised even Cody; they were so deep. By then Quanah was assisting several roadmen as a drummer or poking fire.

The overwhelming scent of sagebrush near Cody as he scoured the landscape for the lost sheep filled his nostrils. That same scent, mixed with cedar and other sweet herbs, hung on Quanah after he left the tipi, the last time they were together. Quanah stood outside the tipi in early morning dew, wrapped in a red and blue robe, lifting his arms to the bright sun, the hem of the robe fluttering in warm early breeze and his form was filled with light; it was airy and transparent.

Such promise...

Today Quanah was gone. He fluttered away.

It made Cody turn around and around at the time, his eyes searching the air and the ground around him. Lost lamb. Lost sheep.

Those pictures of Quanah ended abruptly and earth and sky loomed up before him, solid and close, blocking his view of what lay on the other side of the hill. The sun, its heat and circling shadows on floating ground was all there was, what Quanah came out of, went back into.

There's no going back… Streams don't run that way…

The next new moon, someone came to Cody asking for a ceremony.

"That can be done," he nodded and turned all his thoughts toward praying for the young man for whom it would be held.

When another of Cody's grandsons stood tearfully before him later and asked, "Isn't it too soon?" Cody looked him in the eye and said firmly, "Get ready to help this young man. That's what I am going to do. Come over and support me. We must go on."

The grandson before him, in an outpouring of grief rushed at him and said angrily, "Grandfather, some people are talking about our loss. Someone said it happened because Quanah followed the peyote road."

Cody swallowed that. He put a large hand on his grandson's shoulder and looked at the tears streaming down his grandson's face. He spoke very slowly as if he had all the time in the world to watch what became of those tears.

"Grandson died because people die. Sometimes we are aborted before birth, sometimes we go in infancy, sometimes in childhood, sometimes in adolescence, sometimes in adulthood, and sometimes in old age We expire, and though we do all we can to keep it, breath leaves us."

Today so many of us think dying is wrong...

The missing sheep cavorted around greasewood toward the corral, bleating; its legs splayed out. From the corral, sheep dogs ran toward Cody. Their paws made a string of earthy sounds.

There wasn't a day that passed when he didn't miss Quanah. He had let him go, however.

Life is that... Letting go... Holding on...

He set aside thoughts of his departed beloved grandson and wondered about Dusty. Chee said his son, Dusty, was standing at the edge of a deep cliff. Cody heard the strain in the old timer, but he knew what the old man was made of too.

Generations...

Chee

THE DAY OF the ceremony arrived and it was where everything had led, the path he kept clearing. He was outside making preparations. Though alone right then, he felt the force of all his children, the pull of each one's life separate from his, separate from their mother. He was in a great swirl of family movement and convergence.

Unexpectedly, an incident he hadn't thought of in at least a decade rushed at him.

Another woman came between me and the children's mother once...

She was one of Susie's distant relatives, a younger woman with dark smoky eyes and some daring. They met at one of the summer events.

Her name was Rita, she with the inviting smile, and love of chatter.

Susie said of her after their reunion, "We haven't seen each other since we were girls. Back then she was awkward and silly, and kind of quiet, with a mouth full of missing teeth. Now, what a beauty and such a talker!"

Honestly, he agreed about her devastating beauty, but kept his opinion to himself.

Susie told the younger woman. "Come visit us. You are always welcome."

Rita appeared perhaps six or seven times whenever he was around. He really didn't notice, until summer passed and late autumn came to cool everyone down and Susie voiced that observation.

Rita made her way through throngs of people to hang onto Chee's hand longer than necessary. Her hand was smooth and clingy.

"My cousin is different now. She doesn't seem interested in visiting with me as much as with you."

He always greeted the younger woman warmly and with a joke or two whenever they met, and he didn't change that even after Susie's comment.

Rita went so far as to tease him while he visited with other men and tried to get him to talk at length. Standing face to face and close enough that their arms touched, she smiled bewitchingly at him, breathing on him, and Chee discovered he had to turn away. She was daring, indeed. Most women didn't behave that way openly in those years.

"Yes," he said to himself, accepting that there was something to what Susie had earlier suggested.

One afternoon, after Rita spent the morning with them, Susie asked him directly but so quietly, "Do you find her appealing?"

He narrowed his black eyes cautiously at her; she sat looking right at him, unblinking. This was a far cry from the fifteen-year-old girl he married, who only answered "yes" and "no." He thought her question over and tossed it away.

Some questions never have good answers...

Sammie and Wayne played nearby. Their voices hovered in the background.

He turned and headed for the field. Hunter, Sammie, and Wayne followed. Much later, he returned sweaty and tired, trailed by the boys.

He asked, "What shall we do with the rest of the crops this year? What we will not use, before they spoil?"

Susie made a suggestion. Then she picked up Austin, and started rocking him to sleep.

While I worked in the field that day, the sternness of my relatives on the marriage day returned... Their words were fitting right then... What I didn't understand earlier as a young man, I understood well that day out there...

"My children, there will be all kinds of temptations..." Warning.

In the foresight of that marriage day counsel, he found guidance.

Susie always had a hold of me... When the long spider lashes closed... When she lay down beside me...

The smoky-eyed young woman disappeared into the dry brown hills.

"You have a family here," Susie said that night. She looked shorter, smaller, as she walked toward him in the lamplight, holding Austin at her breast. Her hair was loose, stringing down to her heels, damp. She looked wildly free and soft that way. The other children slept scattered about them.

"Yes," he said, "My family is dear to me, too."

I meant it completely... Though in our generation some men still had more than one wife, I was satisfied...

With his children looking to him that day in the field, he considered each of them. The boys were following his lead and Mary was with Susie at the house. They sat together under a massive cottonwood and its gentle rustling boughs swept their laughter to him.

All their voices, and each one's presence, soothed him, and promised something.

One of the boys tugged at him and held up a chapped

arm filled with burrs on the sleeve. Chee pulled them off, wiping away blood with a calloused hand.

The boys were haphazardly clothed. Their pant legs were too short and that drew the eye to their shoes, ripped and curled at the soles.

All of them, the children, and Susie and he, were ragged. Their poverty was another burr stinging them. They shook their clothes vigorously; the burrs hung on tightly.

He stopped long enough to sit, catch his breath, and see how much work still had to be done. All the melons they collected were piled up at the end of each row. One of the boys brought water in a jug and Chee poured it on his own face first and then on each of them. Water streaked their dirty faces and they laughed hilariously and uncontrollably at one another's funny face.

He selected a melon from under one of the vines and cut it open, putting a slice in each of the boys' rough hands. Watching them clown and play after all the work, he knew without doubt that he loved their sweat and dirt on their hands and clothes.

I never forgot the hardship of that summer and I saw the faces of my mother and father look at each other across their lives in seasons past...

Uneasiness between him and Susie had made summer and fall very difficult on their family. They had conquered all obstacles they had ever met, together, just the two of them. Conflict with one another exhausted the whole family and left both of them feeling defeated. Susie talked about a loss of energy and he didn't enjoy his field as he usually did.

Through the years, he was always on guard, unconsciously and consciously. The push and pull of family and internal and external forces were unmistakable. Now, here he was, face to face with more seasons propelling him onward.

The children shot up like plants in his and Susie's field. Before he knew it, he was old age itself, and only a couple of his offspring elected to stay at the family homestead.

The births of all the children, Hunter to Curtis, spanned how many winters? Thinking of each one, a face appeared in his mind to match each name.

All, but one, were married. Hunter was over sixty and he lived in the nearest border town about twenty miles away. Mary also lived in town but not the same one in which Hunter lived. Sammie died in an automobile accident when he was a mature man. He had just moved to California, to work there, when it happened. He left behind children from two marriages and two grandchildren as well. His grandchildren visited Susie and Chee on holidays.

Nearly eighteen years had passed since Sammie died. Where he and Susie had put him into the ground was a faint spot in evening light.

Wayne married an older woman later than his brothers and sisters married, at the age of thirty, and made his living breaking horses and riding the rodeo circuit until he had broken almost every bone in his body at least twice. Then he retired and spent most of his time raising cattle.

Austin recently celebrated a birthday with a peyote ceremony for himself. He was always sought after in the community. After some college in California earlier in his life, in a surprising twist, he suddenly put that life away and came home. He apprenticed himself to a local singer, and for several months thereafter, learned all he could about three short ceremonies.

As a young man, he brought home with him a California Indian woman who stayed almost two years, but he admitted to the family soon after, "She's always lonesome for Los Angeles."

Eventually, one windy day, she told Austin apologetically, "I packed my bags and I'm catching a ride to the bus station." They hugged each other tightly and she left, waving a slender hand from the car window.

"I saw it coming," Austin admitted to his father. They had been outside working, trying not to struggle against strong wind.

Then Austin ended up marrying a woman from over the hill. Lily. They had four children. One died in infancy.

Dusty migrated to Albuquerque then Phoenix to Salt Lake City and Denver. He was with a different woman each move. Finally he met the one who was now his wife but he still hadn't settled very well.

I told Susie all along the children will be all right... They know where home is....

Seasons went on and he and Susie waited on Dusty to find whatever he thought would make him whole; they went long distances to check his progress several times. Those journeys were always at Chee's suggestion.

Each time Dusty opened the door to find them standing there, out of place in sprawling urban spots, he always showed genuine pleasant surprise and held each of them in his arms for a long time. He made extra efforts to show his life was under control. They looked over the places he called home and returned his embrace before departing.

It's hard to be critical of our own... Whether they are our children or other relations... Out of affection we hesitate to criticize...

Keith was a politician and a natural peacemaker, often called upon to settle local and family disputes. He had the largest family with seven children and his wife was a teacher at nearby junior high school.

Sarah, too, was a teacher. Ross often helped her with

finances because she had three small children and her husband had moved on.

Ross was a talented artist, starting out drawing in dirt and sand. By the time he was thirty-five, he was selling his paintings for a few hundred dollars apiece.

Chee couldn't imagine the amount of money everyone said Ross's paintings brought. He and Susie, however, did admire the shiny truck he drove home on his last visit, walking around it and gingerly stroking the interior. They had never owned such a thing.

Right now Curtis wasn't married. He had been, but his wife didn't want to live out here. "Too lonely," she said. She wanted to live in town, so Curtis rented a house over there but it was too late. She was gone right after. Now Curtis stayed here most of the time but kept the house in town. "In case," he said to his brothers, with a laugh. "In case..."

Life goes on no matter our situations... My own father outlived my mother... Up to the day he died, he maintained his own hogan...

The old house built by Hunter and Chee had been expanded considerably and other buildings stood up around it. None of them had plumbing but they had electricity. Water was hauled from a short distance away. That was usually done by Curtis and Austin, since Chee's body didn't permit that kind of work anymore. Curtis and Austin also brought wood, the family cooking and heating source. Their power line came in the late 60s.

The 1930's and 40's were the most difficult for Susie and Chee. All sheep herds were reduced and money was scarce. Each day they hung onto a few livestock and their field. Each day they did was a victory. They now valued both their livestock and land more than ever. Both of those things and their work had brought them stability.

Cycles complete themselves and start anew... My time will be up soon and I will go where elders go... Old people say to not think about it...

He looked down at hard ground, still guarding his steps to the house from the tipi ground. This was the route he walked every day to keep his joints oiled, as much as he could. His eyes swept over the hard buildings to his left and to his right. He had put those up with his bare hands, with long working days, and with some help from caring people. He paused.

He looked up at the soft, hypnotic sky and back toward the buildings again. Both spurred him.

The force of his family was real. His sons. His daughters. His grandchildren. His great grandchildren.

The offspring will always be tested... Each generation must prove itself...

Their lives were different nowadays; some of his offspring lived in apartments in town and had never seen stars from a desert bed. Some had no fields of their own. He saw the irony and let out a little groan.

It's progress they say...

He felt all his children, close and far.

Hunter, Austin, and Keith followed the peyote road. Mary's husband was part Anglo and Navajo; they joined a Christian church in town. Wayne didn't go to any church or ceremonials anymore, like Ross. Sarah went to both peyote and Navajo ceremonials, and a Christian church, too. Curtis had never been to a peyote meeting in his life although opportunities were there and neither was church a part of his life. His knowledge of traditional ceremonials was minimal, too. He'd lived in the midst of them his entire life.

Families break in many ways... It can easily happen, quietly unseen or painfully loud and clear...

Susie

SHE AND CHEE didn't press their children to be like them or unlike them. Family life however was strongly pressured by far away government. Their offspring grew up in boarding schools, and with a rash of machines and factories, and fast transportation. Foreign wars had a long reach, calling three of them. What Susie did to counteract all that sway was to remain herself and try not to grab at every new thing or idea that went by.

Work... Follow day's cycle...

Preparing for Dusty's ceremony, there was a lot to be done. She'd just overseen the butchering of a sheep and was washing pans and knives in the early morning with some visiting grandchildren. They were telling about their schooling.

She looked toward the corral, recalling the first departure of her offspring for school. The family had lived over there when it happened. She made no comment. Her face was blank. Emotion from that day had long since been attended.

Her grandchildren and great grandchildren knew nothing of how school began for all of them. They thought it had always been the way it was and that it would stay this way from now on.

Hanging dish towels to dry on the line, she saw Hunter and Chee at the tipi ground, smoothing it down, making it firm. She realized how long it had been in that location. Something else came to mind, too.

The first time we used medicine together... I and Chee...

She had no knowledge of the ceremony when she and her young man got together. Few people did. Then in a bold move, over a decade later, some local men brought it out in the open.

Chee explained, "They want to use this sacred herb, along with our elders' teachings, to go into the future. They want to use it to survive. They want to do it right. For generations, for hundreds of seasons, we've chosen our own way."

He had been going to that ceremony alone, with other men...

"Each time, something is gained and I feel at ease there, even though we sit all night and the next day my body might be tired."

Insights he had there about himself, his life and family were quietly penetrating, at least in the way he described them.

"They won't mean anything to others."

One day Susie heard him talk about a future ceremony and she said decisively, "I'll go, too."

That evening they walked to the prayer place nearby.

She stayed awake the whole night because it was required of everyone, unlike other ceremonies. At every prayer meeting since, she was always challenged to stay awake and keep her attention on the matter set before them.

In some ways the new ceremony was like older ones and yet not...

Everyone sat on the ground and sometimes leaned against the walls, though leaning was discouraged. About fourteen people were present; she was one of three women. In those days, women seldom went.

Halfway through, a disturbance was heard outside as the roadman sang. The fireman rose from his place and went out. It was dim inside, before electric lights. When he returned he looked disheveled. His long hair had come loose and his jacket hung off his shoulder. The roadman kept on singing. The drummer at his side followed that lead, drumming steadily to a rhythmic swish-swish-swish of the rattle in the roadman's hand. When the roadman stopped singing, he looked at the fireman. Both were about to speak.

Suddenly, the door flung open and swung back and forth on a squeaky hinge. A loud thud hit the doorframe. She looked up in surprise.

Men rushed in before the fireman could stop them. Who they were was unclear. They stood just inside the door and looked around. They were dark threatening figures, walking directly toward the ceremonial fire. One of them kicked at the end of the burning crossed logs blocking his way and the logs rolled off one another in all directions. That caused the space to darken even more. A smoking log came to rest in front of Susie.

Another man stepped forward and said to the roadman, "My relatives, I tried to prevent these men from coming here but their minds were set. The two here wanted to come at this time to be sure to catch people here. They say your ceremony is wrong. They say medicine is bad and causes insanity and sexual frenzy. They say it's evil. They say this is not religion. They say you are not being religious."

At an angle in the firelight, his features were blurred but when the man spoke, she knew it was Little Singer who lived about ten miles away. He was perhaps twice as old as

Chee and he was one in the community who preferred older ceremonials to all newer religions gaining footholds there. In his own right, Little Singer was a persuasive speaker, highly regarded because he was reasonable and calm, willing to listen to everyone before he made decisions and gave advice. She had no way of knowing how good or imperfect his English was when pressed to use it.

One white man shouted. "Use of this plant is prohibited. Now get up and clear out!" He waved his arms toward the open door. A strong wind whipped in and the place began to cool.

Like her, most of the people didn't understand him or how he could be there. This place was theirs. Certainly Chee didn't, but the stranger's wild behavior and booming voice told them something very obvious.

The person conducting the ceremony told Little Singer, "Ask him to leave. If he wants to talk, tell him to come back in the morning." The other Navajos with Little Singer understood and stepped backwards; they were unsure what to do next.

Little Singer translated. "These people want you to go. They want to finish their ceremony. They say come back in the morning and they'll talk."

The man who had kicked at the logs told Little Singer, "Tell them what I said earlier. Tell them!"

Little Singer answered, "They already know it."

"Tell them anyway!" the white man yelled. "Tell them I mean business!"

Little Singer assumed his speech-making stance and said calmly, "This one is a messenger from way back east. He came here to meet with our leaders in the hope of putting a stop to your ceremony. He and others don't want you to use it. He says others are going to pass laws so no one will have it. He says this herb causes drunkenness and laziness, and has nothing to do with God. That's why they want to put an end to it."

One of the other Navajos who came with the intruders then stepped forward and said, "This *bilagaana* is right. This herb is no good. You have to listen; he knows what's best for you. The government's going to punish you if you don't listen. I've heard about this herb making Indians do crazy things.

"When you go to school as I did, you learn that we haven't gone very far because we use herbs like this and because of our ceremonials. They hold us back." The speaker's face was all shadow.

"We been worshipping all wrong. Some of us have now learned that we ought to be afraid of that part of us that wants to be this way—because it's bad and disruptive to the *bilagaana* and to our own people. We ought to be afraid of these ceremonies because they keep us in the dark and believing in spirits. The *bilagaana* don't like it. They want us to get on the white man road. I think it's good, what they tell us. They want us to be like them."

The man was younger than Susie and his language was poor. He was a stranger to everyone and didn't say who he was. He mispronounced some words but held the attention of everyone.

The roadman waited after the stranger spoke. Then he looked up at the intruders and said, "Now they must either leave, or sit down and stay until the close of the ceremony." Little Singer nodded and spoke to the white men.

"We go now. You said what you wanted. If you don't want to leave, this man has invited you to stay and join the ceremony."

All turned around and filed out except the white man who spoke earlier and he grew belligerent again, "I'm not leaving! I came here to have my say. I won't go until this group scatters!"

The other white man came back inside and lightly brushed the first one's arm to get his attention. He called out a name, "Come on now. Let's get out of here. This is their place. Besides look at them; they seem okay to me. It's dark but they aren't drunk."

The first one wasn't satisfied. He called Little Singer back inside. "Can you chase these people out?" he asked. "I will take full responsibility!"

Little Singer drew his shoulders back and put a hand on his hip. "I'm one man," he said.

The fire was nearly out. Light was from charcoal only. Those who did not understand English watched and heard the exchange without knowing what Little Singer was being asked to do. One who did understand stepped over the logs to the roadman, and told him. Another participant who also understood English whispered to Chee. Everyone's eyes settled on Little Singer.

Little Singer didn't answer, didn't say a word in either language. He firmly shook his head no, turned suddenly, and walked out a second time.

The first white man started to yell, "Now, see here, Singer, you'll answer for this!"

The second white man urged, "Come on, let's go! There's already been too much trouble over this."

His partner held up a fist, shaking it around. Then he turned and swiftly left, followed by the other. The fireman followed them, too.

How long the exchange took wasn't known, but it happened fast.

After the intruders left, the group inside sat in momentary silence. The roadman was calm and so were his helpers, the drummer and cedar man. The fire-man returned to gather the smoking logs thrown across the ground and he built up the fire once more. A flame rapidly lit the hogan. He went outside to get more firewood. When he came back, he said, "They've all gone but one. He wishes to stay."

The roadman looked up curiously and nodded. He raised his hand, motioning the newcomer to enter. Little Singer then appeared in the doorway.

They went on with the ceremony and in the morning they waited for the others to return, but no one showed. Little Singer told them all what had been said and why the two white men had come so boldly into their area and into that ceremony. It was a strange and unlikely event.

What happened that night showed how things are...

As she and Chee walked home the next day, he asked, "What do you say?"

Susie stopped and looked at him. She had no words and started walking again.

"Come on," he said, "What do you say?"

She shrugged and answered hesitantly, hesitantly because she didn't reason and speak the way he did. He was a man; she was a woman. They had different views, different ways of being in the same world.

"Medicine and this ceremony are feared by some. Maybe they're too new. But there are men such as you, with good sense, who see and know something else."

That was the extent of her comment. She did have one question but held it back for a while. Her other questions were gone by then or had answered themselves.

"Are you surprised by he who said that medicine will hold the people back?"

It was a clear day and Chee stood on the ridge they were getting ready to go down, surveying their homestead in the distance.

"I heard that before, but I trust medicine and this ceremony more than that kind of talk. And it's not so that medicine is new. I'll tell you why."

He told her a story he had heard at other prayer meetings about how long the herb had been among tribal people.

That wasn't the only time something threatening happened... Another time, Chee was rounded up...

It happened after the first incident with Little Singer. It shouldn't have happened at all, and later, people involved claimed that it really didn't, or it was a bluff, or mistake.

Chee went to a prayer meeting about four miles away. It proceeded in the usual way, but when everyone came out in the morning, a policeman, waited outside, sitting on horseback. At that time there weren't many police and two other men were with him.

The policeman held a rifle across his saddle and called out, "My relatives, I've come over because of the herb that's being used here. I won't harm you, but come with me. We must talk this over."

The few who came out of the meeting outnumbered the policeman and his companions. They could have wrestled them and ended the matter right then, but they didn't. They merely glared at them for a few minutes and then the participants shrugged and waited.

A wagon was there. "Climb on!" Right then, two or three of those who had been in the meeting just turned and walked away, went back to their homes. The rest went along with the round-up though. Chee recalled a mild threat if any more of them left.

So much about life never gets told... Life's too large...

The wagon was driven to a log building a short distance away.

Chee told her later, "I watched what was happening as we rode away. My companions all were watchful, too. Behind our wagon, the policeman rode and other people followed. There was a lot of talk back and forth. It was a short ride but a hard one, too. It stung."

As an afterthought, he added, "Oh, in the wagon there was a woman..."

When they arrived about midmorning, the group was aimed toward one door. They filled the small room. They ate from jars and talked among themselves.

Chee told her what they said. Each had a view of what had happened to them. No two thought in exactly the same way. Some had gone to school and the others hadn't. But there was no further talk between their group and the policeman who wanted them over there.

Later, all of them left when their families began to gather outside, but not before stern advice was given.

"This is your fault. You people don't listen to *Washingdoon*. This is what can happen. You were brought here for your own good. So you can see how strong others are."

Chee listened well to the younger man doing the talking and went out the door.

He came out, brushing at his black hat, and climbed on his own wagon and patted Susie's hand reassuringly.

Hunter told him, "Your horse is home. He came back by himself."

Most of the ride home was silent. Susie was thoughtful. Hunter and Chee were deep in thought as well. It was midday.

Then Susie spoke, "They said this might happen."

"Yes," Chee agreed. "It will make our way harder to follow."

And with that, he had answered another question, the one she'd withheld after the first incident, the one she didn't need to voice after all.

That was the only time Chee went through that, though Washingdoon and the policeman and others said it didn't happen...

This many seasons later, those memories still had bite. Nevertheless, she was able to watch them coolly when they came close, able to see their distractions.

Her and Chee's life together was incredibly fruitful. All their children made their own homes now. The childhood each one had so many seasons before had run its course. All she and Chee could do now was to be present as long as they could. With the tiniest bit of sentiment about this time of their lives, she slowly walked toward their tipi ground and sat down on a rough bench there.

I don't know how many times Chee put up a tipi for his children...

As for the long ago agreement with Chee, it was as fresh today as it ever was. Admittedly, there were times in the childbearing years when motherhood seemed to outweigh and displace it, but now that those years were behind her, their agreement loomed larger than ever ahead of her.

Oaths...

Mary

SHE GLARED AT her granddaughter, saw a determined young woman meet her icy gaze. Coral was a serene twenty-year-old with an infant nursing at her breast, making contented sounds. Approaching sixty, Mary didn't show any serenity today, seldom did, but her will matched Coral's and anyone else who contested her.

"Yes!" she said forcefully.

Coral calmly looked her quickly in the eye, merely indicating no, and in that way had the last word. Mary's whole body flexed.

It shouldn't be this way... It's because of Lester...

He sat woodenly at her side. She turned toward him.

"You want to say something?" Her voice was high, almost desperate.

They faced each other on the edge of their chairs in their familiar hostile way and she saw for the umpteenth time their contrariness and how their initial differences had deepened into chasms over forty years.

At one time she was convinced they shared more things in common than differences, and of course likenesses pulled them to one another at the beginning. Later on, it became plain that the similarities were only on the surface of their lives.

He deceived me, but I held back when I found out...

Those differences went to the heart and bone of who they were. For instance, she was never able to contain herself in trying situations, like the one now. Emotions churned and splattered internally, and then she released them outwardly. In the meantime, she put on an impassive face.

Lester seemed to hate her displays since he couldn't bend and loosen up with anyone. His children may have been the exceptions, and then only partially, in rare instances.

Why did we get together in the first place? What did we find in each other?

In appearance she was slightly overweight with a jiggle to her walk, and Lester was a pole without a drop of fat. He was a slow mover and she was hasty and impatient. Their reflections in the rectangle mirror across the room didn't reveal the inner things but did show her red complexion, the color of sandstone, and short graying waved hair her fingers raked when she was in a hurry. Lester was white with long dark hair hanging over his shoulders. In contrast to her empty face, Lester always wore a pained expression.

She was a whirlwind talker; Lester kept his mouth zipped in front of others including his children. She loved to quote scripture, or to sing hymns to herself. She had a strong voice though at times it could be shrill. Her favorite biblical passage was, "There shall be no other gods before me." She quoted it daily, holding one finger in the air, waving it back and forth in the face of any listener. That habit worked its way into almost every conversation. Whenever she spoke and acted like that, she saw Lester's green eyes look down and he started coughing as if something was stuck deep in his throat, and wouldn't come out.

Lester never read—the Bible or anything else. And he

didn't make enough conversation these days for her to know if his mind worked or not.

I throw up my hands Lord!

Lester started coughing. He stood abruptly to go sit outside. He spent a lot of time there whenever the house was divided. After the children had grown and departed, the yard became his refuge. Its silence, spaciousness, and solitude won him, over her objections.

Lester could be as quiet as a stone but could cuss pretty good, too, between coughing spells, long shocking phrases that would raise eyebrows in the toughest bar anywhere, but thankfully only she was exposed to that side of him now. It didn't happen often. His two extremes were so annoying when she wanted him to say something thoughtful and not just sit as he did now—as if he didn't have a tongue at all, or else go too far, saying too much.

Nowadays Lester walked a straight line, guarded his thoughts and speech carefully, but occasionally he slipped and said clearly, "shee-it!" If Mary was there, she glared at him until he became as small as a mouse and disappeared. She wasn't able to pinpoint when this started to happen exactly. Suddenly it was obvious and set, and she accepted it.

Oh, God, he's weak...

Increasingly over years he moved further away from her; finally he left her alone to make decisions for the family but he hadn't always been this way.

What happened?

Coral hummed softly, rocking the dozing infant in her arms.

She didn't trust herself with Coral. She might go too far and say something far more destructive, or mean, than she ever had before, or she might become physical.

I'm capable of it... If Lester had been stronger or more talkative or more religious or more loving to the grandchildren, maybe Coral's decision would be different...

She wanted to pounce on him. She got up and followed him.

He sat on the porch in a rocking chair, not surprised when she came out and settled beside him. He cleared his throat and waited.

Glaring at him, she searched her vocabulary for the most stinging words. Her brown eyes were glittery cold and under the freeze, his pale skin turned whiter until all the blood was squeezed from his veins. Then he did what he always did; he began to shrink before her eyes. Immediately he was as small and timid as a mouse.

Whenever he does this I want to grab his tail and throw him far out into space!

She couldn't find words she wanted; none were powerful enough. It was a tall order and she was unable to think because of Coral. That, combined with rage at Lester, was too much to bear. She forced down a scream. Her eyes darted from Lester to the street beyond the fenced yard and he promptly returned to his normal size.

After a minute or two she regained control of herself. Then Coral's words bounced back and her blood began to bubble, boil.

She'd worked hard to prevent her family from doing exactly what Coral was choosing.

"It's a dead-end!" she warned.

Rub all that away... Forget it...

"I'm saying and doing this for each of you," she told them through the years. "It's for your own good. You don't know what it's like to live in a home without water or electricity. You don't know what it's like to be humiliated for speaking your own language, or not having nice clothes and things. It hurts."

Lester never said anything at those critical times, his tongue was completely gone.

I might as well have been without him during the times when I alone steered the children in the direction I wanted... Right or wrong...

His rocking chair started again. The floor boards creaked rhythmically. Abruptly she realized that his silence through most of the years was probably the best thing; he would have disagreed with her if he was more talkative, and then, where would they all be?

"More confused than ever!" she answered herself.

Lester looked at her as if she was out of her mind whenever she spoke aloud to herself. He stared that way at her now, as if on the very verge of something.

With absolute certainty then, she knew she could never really tolerate him speaking his mind.

Would his absence have been better than his silence after all?

She shook her head, no. She wanted him to be near and she couldn't face being alone. Though no words passed between them and the house was mute most of the time, she had her way.

The back and forth thinking was weary.

11

Before her first love, now so many years behind her, she'd been so open and pliant.

Hopeful...

Close to her family then, she attended all their events and ceremonies, and knew she had a place there. That certainty was soothing during childhood and girlhood.

Her face flushed. She forgave herself; that tranquil time of closeness and certainty was way before she accepted that her family's way was not good. Her mother and father had false gods. Today, she felt such enormous relief someone later told her those two truths and that she came to be saved and rescued from her earlier fate — the fate of her mother and father. It was painful knowledge and separated her from them for good.

What she had now was best. She was approaching old age and her children usually brought direction; even Lester made her invincible whether he intended it or not.

They met when she was twenty, recovering from first love gone wrong. Those were the only two loves in her life and they were worlds apart, so much so that she was a different young woman with each of them.

She saw herself before she met Lester.

I was soft and doughy then... Girlhood and love made me soft...

She was in a large boarding school, where she first learned to read and write. Fortunately many others were in the same situation, older and away from their families for the first time. They all mixed with other tribal people not their own, and with others who weren't Indian at all. It was a new way of living, theirs to take, though before then, such behavior was not encouraged. For her, the new experience was happily received and before she knew it, her family had nothing she wanted anymore.

Physically, she *was* softer; slender and wispy, a new blade of grass. Long thick black hair and clear liquid brown eyes were features she liked best about herself. She thought she would look like that forever.

Her closest friend was Winona Turtle, a mixed blood from a very distant and unfamiliar people. Winona was younger, reed-like in stature, and she had an older brother named Jesse. They came from a very traditional background and spoke their own language. Their father died when they were children and their mother remarried two or three times but none of her men accepted Winona or Jesse. Their paternal grandparents rescued them from further rejection.

We three were so innocent...

One holiday Winona took Mary home. Just as they arrived outside a large dark cabin, Jesse came straggling in from a small field. He took off his hat, brushed back his wet hair from his forehead, and Mary felt her first jolt of love. He was about twenty-five and a foot taller than she. He strode right up and asked, "Who's this, Winona?" Then he winked at Mary, not at all shy. Right then she memorized his quick smile and gray eyes.

Jesse's grandparents gently pushed him out of their way, bustling around, anxious to feed her and make her at home. They were gentle people, speaking with an unfamiliar accent. In the next two days, she shared with them her family history. They were good listeners, stopping her every now and then to repeat a phrase she said in their heavy accent. In turn they told about themselves and tales of their people. Their accent, heavy as it was, did not prevent her from understanding, though it was like listening from under a blanket. She saw Jesse about four times before she left, at breakfast and at evening meals. During the days she helped Winona do chores and evenings were full of memorable stories and wild sounds in the countryside.

It was an unreal time... Too much innocence... Too much expectation...

↟↟↟

My own family drifted further away... It had to happen...

Through the old people, she learned that Winona and Jesse's ancestors previously lived in mountainous country near the eastern ocean for a few hundred years but were chased out by invaders, recently. A leader of those days was Turtle. When they said it, it sounded more like Tuttle.

Winona said, "He was a wealthy man, a learned man. He read and wrote the invaders' language, too. Many of our grandfathers did at the time. They almost had to."

Whatever became of Winona and Jesse I don't know... Some things don't last...

Friendly to the invaders, Turtle was known to defend them and speak on their behalf in the first part of his life until the day came that one of them revealed a terrible plan. "We'll remove all tribal people from their old settlements and exile them." When a few invaders in gentlemen apparel of the period slyly asked Turtle to be an accomplice, he asked, "What? WHAT?"

Out the sides of their mouths, the invaders promised, "A handful of you might be permitted to stay, if you help oust the others. It's the only way."

Turtle winced first, then growled his rage, and looked down at land which bore him. The invaders repeated their offer—to be sure they were fully understood. "At our graciousness and charity, only the most cooperative of you will be permitted to stay among us, on your so-called sacred land."

Winona repeated the words all of them had memorized, and she spit at the feet of those long deceased people.

Then Winona's grandmother said, "In the blink of an eye, Turtle's men grabbed that sly man and threw him down. Then Turtle and his men turned like this and went away from them forever." Her upper torso turned quickly and her chin lifted.

As Mary recalled those evenings with the older Turtles, her own bitterness diminished. So captivated was she again by Turtle's story, after so many years! She heard Turtle and others scuffle with the invaders beside the porch. Her inclination to silently fume was gone.

I thought their story was forgotten...

Winona's grandparents patiently explained to her— and as it turned out, to anyone else who would listen— Turtle's mind. They spoke alternately, softly and slowly, and their accented speech was very stirring in moonlit nights when crickets, too, made themselves heard in choruses around them.

"We want you to know his thinking."

"The ground coveted back then won't ever be owned by a single man; too many lineages go with it."

"All share it, its summer and winter."

"The thick game and timber were what they wanted. Things they could turn into money."

"When our people told them, 'You kill the land,' they laughed and said, 'It never lived.' "

"On they went, clearing out everything, in an angry and fast sweep. Forests fell in slashing waves, the way game had. Before our people knew it, those things were gone. Nothing was left but lines of shelters for them, who kept trying to make empty land."

Why waste my time on all this?

The story continued on its own; she tried to ignore it. "Our people grieved at the loss: land and life on it. The invaders were blind. Then the ground was broken up and pieces passed down to unrelated land owners."

Mary saw them, the old storytellers, their silhouettes and gestures, talking softly to each other and to the night. Above, lights grew bright and dim.

"From then on, Turtle led some men who didn't want to let go of that place. Even when they were driven off, Turtle vowed, 'I don't give up without fight.'"

"Over a thousand miles, they fought. On foot, stripped of everything, Turtle was one who led our people here."

The old storytellers had power for sure... But it was wasted on me...

She turned to look at Lester again; he carefully ignored her. He was what she had, not her first love, Jesse. This was their life.

She waved away the image of herself as a slim young woman with her innocent desire for love. Because of her youth and expectation, that first romance left her wounded. Nevertheless, she learned something.

It's dangerous... It made me weak... Better to stay far from it... Better not to feel...

She learned that much about herself and a little history which was still haunting, perhaps more so than memories of Jesse.

Winona's grandfather finished the tale, "Here's how Turtle died."

"Days from Indian Territory, Turtle with about twenty others, came upon a small village of bark lodges. Just ghosts were in it, with howling wind. The east houses were empty. Corpses were on the west side. It looked like some died just as Turtle arrived. The bodies showed suffering. In each lodge, it was the same. The people died all together, in the grip of a thing Turtle and his men didn't know. They had no name for it.

"In the last shelter, Turtle stood over rotting flesh and

a terrible truth gashed him. Almost at the same time his followers thought of it, too.

"One of his men let out a loud anguished cry, and ran to Turtle.

"He must have seen the same question in all the men's eyes as they lined up before him.

"He said, 'It's true! We can't return to our people!'

"His men were wounded, simply at his words. Their shoulders dropped and they sucked in air, speechless at such fate."

Who knew such things happen?

"Wind blew on them, moaning. Helpless, they moaned too. But that passed. They squared their shoulders and accepted their fate because Turtle was right.

"'We'll die here with strangers,' he vowed. 'We can't carry this back to ones we love. They should not suffer like this!'

"One of his men shed tears openly—for his grandparents, for a woman and small children, and for himself. He was too young; unlike the others, he hadn't yet lived. After a while though, his tears stopped. The others overlooked his outburst.

"Turtle wanted to send out a warning of the deadly place, but feared it would do more harm than good. In the end, he chose the youngest one among them, he who had shed tears, to carry this sad news to others, but he advised his young messenger to not approach any man too closely. The young man left on foot, the way the band always traveled. Turtle posted scouts on each side of the village to prevent travelers from entering. Then he and his followers began to cover the dead.

"A couple of days passed; burials began, with the wind treating them roughly. More days went and Turtle dared to hope they had escaped, until one of them hit the ground. Turtle noticed that man's absence and discovered him laying face down, too weak to move. He dragged him into the nearest shelter under thick swaying trees the wind flogged.

"How many days it took is unknown but that man's collapse was the sign. The rest tried to guess when they all might be hit. They agreed to destroy the village when the winds went down.

"One by one something struck them. Turtle grew weak, too; his eyes sank into his skull, and his brain must have fogged. One by one, they went into the next world. In death, their faces wore strange colorations and their bodies blew up beyond recognition. Turtle and others buried each man hastily fearing traces of that brutality would linger in the village or go beyond if not destroyed. That was why Turtle decided to burn it; at the same time he watched the winds.

"Soon, only five lived, including Turtle. Two lay in a lodge, but now and then one of them staggered out and stood before Turtle like a wandering ghost. Turtle didn't expect to live much longer either and said he thought of himself as all spirit too."

Was their story untrue?

"Finally there was a lull in the winds and Turtle began to burn the dwellings. Smoke lifted.

"Turtle, with two others, dug their own graves and decided what the last of them would do. By then all were walking skeletons but they forced themselves to dig. Because they were too weak, they helped one another.

"That's what they were doing when the ground shook and they knew horses came at a full gallop.

"'They saw the smoke,' Turtle said.

"He and his men waited to see who the horses would

bring. Three invaders Turtle had earlier known appeared in a screen of smoke. They immediately drew weapons.

"Turtle lifted a weak hand and said in the language of the invaders, 'Stop! There's death here!'

"One of the men on horseback began to yell, 'Yes, there will be death now that we've got you right where we want, Turtle! I swear vengeance on each of you. This time none of you are going to escape!'

"'Wait,' Turtle cried out. 'Look around. Death is already here.'

"One of the others on horseback shouted at the man aiming at Turtle, and said, 'Wait a minute! Look at them.'

"The invaders brought their horses to a standstill. They eyed the smoky silent shelters. One of them rode quickly through the village, in and out of smoke, taking no special notice of the dwelling where two men teetered back and forth between wakefulness and death. Both stood like ghosts there. They were partly air and dust by then, and perhaps it was why they were not seen. The ailing men, however, watched the rider pass and even in their condition, not fully alive or dead, knew that he was an enemy. They were bony, clutching one another for support, but too weak to hold each other up. They toppled to the ground and lay unmoving. They heard the horse trot around them in a circle.

"When the rider skirting the village moved on, one man on the ground lifted his head and felt the other's spirit take leave of the wrecked body near him and rise. The survivor paused to watch the spirit of his companion show itself and then disappear. He heard Turtle and others in the distance but all that was unclear. He crawled toward Turtle and the others. He saw Turtle with his other two men stand before the invaders. Turtle's legs were weak, shaky; he barely stood, swaying under a strong wind blowing smoke. One of those with Turtle grabbed his arms to steady him.

"'They're sick!' one on horseback said. They backed the horses away.

"'True!' Turtle said. 'We're dying; maybe it will be now.'

"One of the men with Turtle spoke in their language.

"The rider who went through the village returned. 'There's no one here,' he said. 'Where's everyone?'

"'Dead!' Turtle answered. 'We came to this place, found bodies everywhere. There were more of us but now they're gone too. One by one we have died. We can't say why but no one in this village escaped. We buried them.'

"Turtle spread his feet wider to support himself. He had difficulty speaking. The men with Turtle spoke to him in their language again, clear enough for the other one on the ground a short distance away to hear their words and understand. His tribesmen stared defiantly up at the men on horseback who aimed at them.

"Turtle said, 'We can't leave this place alive. Look at us. We have vowed to leave death here.'

"Their wasted bodies caused them to look wilder and more dangerous than anyone had ever seen.

"'Now none of you may go either! If you do, you'll take death to all those you meet.' Turtle leaned on the arms of his followers.

"'No!' one of the men on horseback screamed. 'You lie!'

"Our men began to walk toward the horses, dragging their feet but still moving.

"'It's true,' Turtle said. 'Meet your death.'

"The follower on Turtle's right began to chant in his language and that made the men on horseback anxious and angry. One of them turned his horse quickly and struck Turtle's follower in the back of the head with his weapon. He was the first to go down with a loud thud. Turtle and his other follower took no notice but continued to stumble toward the men on horseback. The man on the ground nearby saw one of them turn his gun on Turtle. A minute later a shot resounded through smoke and Turtle lay on the ground. The observer in the distance felt his own heart grow fainter at the sight. He tried to raise himself but couldn't lift a hand or say a word. Wind blew and nearly toppled the last of Turtle's followers left standing. The last man with Turtle squared his shoulders and began to walk very deliberately toward he who shot Turtle, chanting in the old language. That man and Turtle's killer faced each other; the man on horseback firmly fired.

"The three invaders immediately rode away in triumph; they didn't know someone was there. That witness gave himself up to blackness then, and when he awoke, found himself in the care of the messenger Turtle sent to warn others.

"The young man had defied Turtle by choosing not to find any people after all. He had gone all the way back to their old place, but so great was his fear that he took suffering and certain death over there, that he did not go in. His love for his people was too great. The only thing to do was to rejoin Turtle.

"For no reason that our people knew, that young man who acted as Turtle's messenger did not fall seriously ill, but only experienced mild sickness. The witness to Turtle's death also recovered, though his body was marked with that illness the rest of his life. Those two survivors stayed in that village of death a few more days until they were sure they were allowed to live. They buried Turtle and the others, and burned the rest of the village until nothing was left but gray ashes wind scattered before them. Then the two said goodbye to that place and went in search of their kinsmen.

"Those three invaders kept the secret of that deadly place, two died without telling it, but they bragged of killing Turtle. In a moment of weakness and remorse, and on his deathbed, the last of them told the whole story of meeting Turtle and his story traveled back to our people."

She tried to unravel the significance of Turtle's deed.

Haunting...

The story brought back a closeness she enjoyed with her grandmother when she was a child. She felt her grandmother's protectiveness. Of course that changed through time. Nothing stays the same. On the brink of old age now she had yet to understand obstacles and bridges between generations. Winona's grandmother had also told them that Turtle warned of, "A time like this."

Life should be easier now... Each generation has it easier...

"Lester," she said more calmly, "I'd appreciate more advice from you on Coral in the future. You heard what she said. Don't you care?"

Lester began to diminish in size again.

Jesse hadn't ever been that way. He was larger than life. He was present when his grandmother retold the story of Turtle for her. She read Jesse's face as he listened. He must have heard it often enough to have it memorized. It inspired him and he gulped at his formidable ancestor.

She thought of her own tender and protective love for her people and their stories a long time ago. That didn't exist anymore. She was more practical and hard these days. Sometimes stories, like people, were full of flaws.

We see it when we grow older...

She retraced the smooth contours of Jesse's face in her

mind; he was so young and solid. She looked hard at Lester, comparing him to the sensual youth he would never equal.

IV

After hearing their powerful story, Turtle stayed in her mind yet she never knew him. Jesse became Turtle in her heart.

I didn't expect to see him after that... I'd fallen for him though and measured other young men against him ...

Two months went by before Jesse showed up to take Winona home and Mary was happy to see him despite the sad circumstance. Their grandmother had died.

Winona returned to school grieving heavily and care of her grandfather was worrisome. Finally, she collected her things and left for the second time. Later, letters came from her. Soon Winona's grandfather died, too. Very quickly, he was gone. Mary encouraged Winona to come back since Winona was the only one at the house all the time. Jesse often had to work in distant towns.

Surprisingly, she agreed and came back more mature than Mary was then.

The bigger surprise was Winona wanting me to marry Jesse...

"He's alone too much now," Winona complained.

"Maybe that's what he wants," she answered. "He can probably marry anyone he wants."

"Oh, he has girlfriends all right, but none of them are good enough for him. Except you, Mary," Winona said sincerely.

Mary laughed from flattery and embarrassment. "Maybe he's too old for me. Besides I ought to marry into my own people."

A shadow now went over her face at such youthful confession.

Lester was my man... I chose him because he has mixed blood...

Not too long after, Jesse again showed up.

"I brought him with me," Winona said cheerily after making a trip home. "I'm trying to play matchmaker," she whispered into Mary's ear.

Mary was angered. She carefully concealed her feelings about him from the start, though they were best friends. She didn't want to be thrown at him.

He was quiet the entire evening.

"Is there anything wrong?"

"I miss the grandparents," he admitted. "They were all Winona and I had."

"You have a mother, don't you?"

"Yes, but she has her own life," he explained. "We don't know her very well. Winona's all the family I have now."

"I'm sorry. I'm sorry for both of you."

The conversation took a turn there, amusing her.

"How old are you, Mary?"

"I just turned eighteen," she said.

"Do you ever plan on getting married?" He grinned broadly.

"If I find the right person," Mary admitted.

"What about someone like me? Would you marry someone like me?" He was completely serious. His smile was gone and it its place was a thoughtful glance at her.

"I don't know anybody else like you," she said.

"Well, would you marry *me*?" He meant it, his gray eyes studying hers.

"I don't know."

"Think about it," he said. "Tell me soon."

He squeezed her hand while her heart thumped loudly. They walked to her building where he gently embraced her. His arms felt new and good She never felt those feelings for anyone before or after.

Only Jesse felt like that...

She ran up the stairs to Winona's room and asked, "Is this your idea? Did you tell him to ask me to marry him?" She was half excited, half angry.

Winona shrieked and laughed loudly, "No, but I'm so happy he did!" She danced around the room, kicking up her legs, trying to pull Mary along.

Just before the end of the school year, Mary wrote to her mother and father telling them she would not be going back. "I'm planning to go to Jesse's home."

I didn't explain any more than that... Really didn't have to...

V

After her decision to marry, she learned of Jesse's secure place in the community.

That's where it started... He loved them more than me...

On the surface she looked happy. Deep down, she knew trouble was coming.

By the time it happened, she had come into contact with many local people, knew most everyone by sight, including some white and black townspeople. She hadn't legally married Jesse although she did share his house, his food and bed. They planned marriage very soon.

One particular weekend Jesse and Winona were preparing to attend a ceremonial event. Both expected her to accompany them.

Not me... Ever!

She awkwardly refused, walking into town alone instead to purchase some cloth and other small items after Winona and Jesse left.

The store clerk was a tall thin man ever watchful of Mary when she entered. He wore horn-rimmed spectacles that hung loosely on his shiny nose. Perhaps he had spoken a dozen words to her in all her visits.

She overheard him tell some people about the event then being held in the community, "It's devilry I say!"

She stopped to eavesdrop.

Even now I'm able to hear him speak...

"Yes, of course, they are like all the others. They worship idols and this from the more civilized ones! They do it as we speak. That's why the store and town are empty."

He looked around as if he might be overheard and looked directly at Mary. She busied herself by pulling out bolts of cloth and examining them, tiptoeing closer. He whispered loudly, "If you attend any of their gatherings, you can actually see them worship Satan. It's terrible to behold. They speak the language of the devil, not civilized speech."

Mary was entranced. She tiptoed closer carrying a bolt of red print.

"That's why they're so dark. Because they're evil! Why they talk to darkness, to things that aren't there! There must be punishment for the way they are and it's our duty to dispense justice for their kind of savagery."

The clerk's audience, two women and a man, were spell bound. The older woman tossed her head. The man pursed his lips and the second woman rolled her eyes toward the high tin ceiling.

Mary paid for the cloth and other items she needed, bowing her head before the trio standing over her at the counter. The other man took her money and tapped impatiently on the counter. She collected her package and went outside.

On her way back, she reviewed what he had said.

As a younger girl, she came to similar conclusions for different reasons.

Her mother and father couldn't keep their children in shoes. New clothes came once a year. Shirts and pants were always shared and passed down by the boys. Their pants or shirts, or both, were either too small or too large. She pictured them in long and large baggy pants with small, faded shirts. Tight sleeves ended below the elbows instead of at the wrists.

I was lucky... I didn't have to share...

The family lived off a single diet. Later, in school, she fidgeted when others talked about her people and how they lived, especially their poverty. Her face flushed when she admitted that her parents spoke only their native language. After a while, she pulled away from anyone who spoke to her in her first language.

That Winona and Jesse also grew up with a first language not English mattered. She expected their experience to mean the same as hers did. In the meantime, her mother and father had someone write to her for them regularly in English, and they often mailed money to her.

She felt a twinge in her heart and ignored it. Her head pounded.

Lester got up and went in the house.

He always does that... Walks away right after I arrive...

It didn't matter this time because her thoughts were on Jesse. She didn't relive the past because it was too painful and pointless, especially the part about leaving him.

His people mattered more than I did...

Winona wasn't like her at all, advising her like a sister, "Begin to think about your future children and what you'll teach them about our people. Maybe you want to learn our language?" Mary was astonished!

Such an attitude... I couldn't take it... They should have known...

She waited for Jesse to return from the fields and when he did, she picked at him. She slammed heavy pots down and disagreed with both Winona and Jesse over small matters. His gray eyes darkened. His surprise seemed real. The day ended badly. Even Winona looked up with a scowl when Mary said with disgust to Jesse, "You and your people are no better off than me and mine!"

The next day started the same, with Mary shoving away the morning meal Winona prepared. Jesse grabbed his hat and escaped before too long.

"What's the matter with you?" Winona asked in exasperation after he left. "Are you mad at Jessie, or me? What did we do?"

She didn't answer for a while, then found enough courage to ask, "Do you two know witchery? Is that why you go into the community so much?"

Winona's flawless face wrinkled up. "What?" she gasped and stopped dusting the room. She walked to Mary and looked her in the eye. She was about four inches taller than Mary and her eyes were lighter than Jesse's.

"What did you say? Where did you get such an idea?" Winona was shocked , angered, and spoke through gritted teeth.

Mary's own mouth quivered. "I heard the white people in town talk about all of you yesterday, all of you who still want to be Indian. One called your gatherings, devilry. That's witchery, isn't it?"

Winona slumped down into a chair. "They say that about all of us, all Indian people. Are we all bad? Are we all witches?"

Mary hushed. She had seen and participated in many ceremonies but up to then, never thought they were devilry.

Winona's question never left her but she never wanted to hear it from anyone else again.

How did I answer Winona?

"We asked you to go with us. Why didn't you?" Winona questioned.

Mary began to help straighten the room. The conversation went no further, but something changed between Winona and her right then. A heavy line was drawn. Winona drew back from Mary apprehensively, cautious after her accusation. Then in her eyes, Winona and Jesse transformed, just as happened with her mother and father. Their break-up took a few weeks longer.

My mother and father didn't know they were wrong... That their lives were wrong...

She acquired a job in town as a dishwasher and waitress at The Cherokee Room owned by Cherokee Sam who, unsurprisingly, was not Cherokee at all. She never learned how he received his name. His place was visited mainly by townspeople but three Cherokee women worked there with Mary. Cherokee Sam was in middle age, a jovial person who greeted everyone daily with a joke and a deep belly laugh.

At The Cherokee Room, she came into contact with people who were very well to do. That association made her happy and envious. Quickly almost all her time was spent over there rather than with Jesse.

One afternoon she accidentally spilled some warm coffee into the lap of a young woman about her own age. Mary was horrified at what she'd done. The Cherokee Room was full then. The young woman was not injured but spiteful. Mary stammered an apology. The young woman stood up and slapped her face. The young woman turned to Cherokee Sam and said angrily, "You're too good to these people! See what they do to us! The nerve!"

Mary flushed bright red. She turned and ran into the kitchen, tears streaming down her hot face. In the next room Cherokee Sam defended her, but it didn't matter. When her eyes dried, she remembered the young woman's words.

The stupid girl thought we're all the same... She didn't know the difference...

The rest of the afternoon she tried to stay in the kitchen and wash dishes. Later, as she folded dish towels and put them away, she told Cherokee Sam, "This will be my last day here."

He seemed to expect it. He shook her hand and wished her well.

She returned to the house humiliated and lonely. Jesse chopped wood outside and didn't enter the house until it was nearly dark. Winona was setting the table when he came inside. The house had been quiet those days even when they were all there together. Winona didn't look up when Mary sat down near her.

During their meal later, Mary said, "I've decided to leave. This is not what I thought it would be. I want something else. More than this."

Jesse stopped eating and looked across the table at her and then at Winona.

"It's not that I don't care about what happens to you, Jesse, because I do," she continued in a pleading voice. "We're just too different. You don't want anything else than to be here, living the way your people have always done. There's a lot more than this."

Her eyes were teary and she sniffled.

Jesse pushed his plate away and asked, "When? When will you go?"

"Tomorrow," she answered.

After the meal, there was awkwardness among them. Finally, Winona left the room.

"I'm sorry," she said and tried to put her arms around Jesse. He pushed them off.

"I kept hoping you could learn to accept what is," Jesse said as he calmly but firmly held her away. "If this is your decision, I agree with it. This place, my home, my people, and I deserve more."

Jesse made a bed on the floor. He tossed and turned and then came his soft snore.

There was confusion that night, wanting Jesse but not wanting what he wanted and how he lived. She almost got up and went to him and told him that she changed her mind. She conquered those urges. Exhausted, she finally closed her eyes.

The next day Jesse was gone when she sat up in bed. Winona was in the kitchen doing laundry. When Mary finally came out of the room, packed and ready to go, Winona said, "You're losing something good. Jesse's a fine man and he loves you for sure. But make no mistake, he loves this place and his people more."

She poured Mary a cup of coffee and said without the slightest hint of anger anymore, "Jesse's gone. He's not coming back until you leave. As much as he cares, he understands what you said last night is true, and truth's stronger than any of us. He said to go, be on your way, and he'll always try to think only good of you."

I haven't looked back... Who would want to?

Leaving the house, a flurry of birds chirped happily on the roof and ground. They flew away in a shiny swirl and Mary made sure to hold her head high as she left that place and time behind.

vii

At age twenty-two, she met Lester.

I felt old by then...

He was so different in those days. He wore a dark mustache which was very becoming. From time to time he ambled into the diner with other members of a large construction crew where she worked, always carrying something to read in his back pocket or tucked under his arm. It was a pleasant surprise to learn that he understood what others said to her over morning coffee.

"You're one of us after all?" she asked when he stayed longer to read a minute or two, or to listen to the old radio sitting high above them.

"Part," he answered. He had a way about him that was very independent.

"From where?" she asked.

"Here," he said looking over his shoulder and lighting a cigarette.

Three months later Lester moved in with her and the next year, she had the first of five babies, all girls.

At the start she was attracted to his candid perspective on things, especially himself and his life. "I'm a lone wolf.

I make it on my own rules." It was a rough masculinity that he displayed so well.

Realizing it, she let out a small bitter laugh and then her laughter grew loud and harsh at the joke played on her.

Life does play tricks...

In their first years together, it wasn't so bad. He worked steady and he enjoyed a drink now and then. Mary dressed herself up too and went with him for a while. After a few months she gave it up because he often bullied her on his sprees. Periodically he threatened to leave.

"I can find a better woman anywhere," he liked to say after a couple of rounds. Then, he sobered up and forgot everything he said and did while he was drinking. He may have actually carried out his threats about other women because she heard rumors from the few acquaintances she had in the neighborhood. She buckled under those threats but was determined to not go back to her mother and father.

A little church stood a couple of blocks from their four room apartment. She passed it often and found herself wondering how it looked inside. The last time she had been in a church was at school where attendance was forced for all students there. She always went; she never had to be disciplined for not going.

One Saturday after receiving a paycheck from the diner, she went back to the apartment to discover her girls alone and hungry. Lester was gone. There was no food. The place was dirty. The girls' clothes were scattered everywhere. She cleaned and dressed the girls and they all walked to the nearest food store. On the way back with a sack of groceries in her arms, Mary's feet hesitated in front of the church. One of the two doors swung open just at that moment. Encouraged, she led them to the open door; her youngest daughter clung to her skirt. She peeked inside and walked down the aisle, the little girls followed along. The long windows had colored crosses set in the panes. There was no sound anywhere except their footsteps.

She slid onto a long bench. The little girls sat down next to her. She put down her sack and a sadness and disappointment came loose. Tears ran in streams down her face. The girls were alarmed; one came over and put a small arm around her. Another brought a hymnal and said, "Look, a book." Mary turned the pages of the hymnal while tears kept flowing. There was something in her past making her feel this way, but she didn't know what. Images of church and school came to her, the print dresses she made for Sundays when she was in school.

Nearly an hour later, she was a new person. She had cried a flood of tears. Drained and renewed, she went home and cooked for the children.

She recalled the relief she felt for the new beginning.

I hoped it would fix everything... It helped a lot...

When Lester came back about midnight, she was sound asleep. It had been such a long time that she had permitted herself to go to bed early when he was out. She habitually walked the floor, waiting for the knob to turn on the door, but not that night. He tried to get her out of bed.

"Damn it, Mary," he said, "Get up and cook. I'm hungry!"

She ignored him and that made him angry. "Oh hell," he muttered, "Damn woman!"

The little girls woke and watched him stagger around. They heard him cuss at Mary and then the girls all climbed into one bed together.

The next day Mary got up early the way she did as a child, and she greeted the rising sun. Excited as a child too, she made a big breakfast; the smell of food woke the girls.

"Let's go to Sunday school, my children," she said.

"What's that?" one asked.

"You'll see," she answered, going to find clean clothes for them.

Church became her refuge. Peace and serenity she hadn't known for a decade filled her.

She started to grow stronger than Lester then. It took him a long time to catch on and when he did, it was too late.

I only wanted to be strong enough to survive... That shouldn't have affected Lester the way it did... After all, the strength I wanted was for him as much as me...

vIII

For years she and the girls went to church by themselves and Lester made them pay for it. As long as he was drinking he was physical and loud. When church came between them, his first actions were hostile and he was bitter. Three times he actually struck out and her face turned purple.

Doesn't matter... I overcame all of it...

She took it almost gratefully. She felt like a blessed person, one whose ability to endure great suffering lifted her from a fragile everyday life, and truly made her look toward rewards in the hereafter for putting up with it. Besides that, if she didn't accept the situation, she had only one place to go.

"Come to church with us," she always replied when he asked her to rub his back or for something to ease the pain that was starting there.

His mean behavior didn't end until he couldn't drink anymore. When his body refused another drop and there was no one to help but her, he took a long hot bath and put on the church clothes she had purchased for him a little at a time over a couple of years. Then he followed her and his teenaged daughters to Sunday school.

It took years to happen. After that, she built their entire lives around church. It appeared to suit everyone, but Lester acquired an unexplainable cough and he actually shriveled in size. They spent little time with other people and she took the leading role in the family while he pulled back and became submissive and mute. After that there was only one thing left to do, cut off all relations with brothers and sisters. Communication with her mother and father hung by a thread.

Neither Lester nor she spoke of his drinking sprees and tirades anymore to anyone. It was as if those and all the years didn't occur. Between him and her, occasionally, she found it necessary to remind him of the most shameful moments.

Their daughters had gradually accepted their new father when he joined them at Sunday school.

My God! They should have been pleased...

They were and they weren't. They were puzzled. The way their mother and father turned away from each other nowadays was especially confusing. When those instances happened they looked at her questioningly. Furthermore, their father's shrinking body and coughing fits didn't reflect the man they knew as children, a tall and robust person, who stood up to anyone. When one of them eventually said it, "Where's my real daddy anyway?" in a wistful and searching way and they began to share their memories of him as a younger man, Mary flounced away from all of them.

Their lives were spent on the edge of the border town; they never ventured too far into their own land or uptown.

Doesn't matter... Haven't missed anything... This is how it's going to be to the end...

All their daughters were grown and gone now. They had seven grandchildren and two great-grandchildren. She never dreamed she could love anyone as much as she did them. She had personally seen to it that all were raised in church, and most spoke only English. The only time she and Lester took them to her mother and father was at Christmas. Thanksgiving was spent with Lester's relatives.

IX

How in the world did we lose Coral?

Coral and Lester, granddaughter and grandfather, were laughing inside the house. Hearing them, anger welled up once more.

They were always so close. Coral spent most of her time with Lester whenever she was around.

When Coral was a newborn, Lester brought home what looked like a peach colored doll dress in a white box for her. White lacy ruffles trimmed the hem and sleeves; it was a couple of sizes too big. The dress had a matching hat. He gave them to Mary and she scolded him for spending money on such frilly things and for not knowing the right size. The dress stayed in the box for a couple of days. When Lester put them on Coral over the clothes she already wore, the baby was completely swallowed up, but she grabbed at the ruffles and hung onto them.

When she was a bit older but still a child, she often sat at his side and held his hand, listening seriously to every single word he said. Lester adored Coral because of that. They acted like they were the only two people in the world.

Mary disapproved.

Too much equality... Too much laughter...

She frowned and went inside.

Austin

ONE EVENING HE might find himself making his way under neon lights and through beams of perilous traffic in big cities and in the following evening be standing in wide open space where electricity was still uncommon and traffic was light or nonexistent. One night he interacted socially in a distant place, thoroughly enjoying the laughter and friendship of a handful of people from that world, and a night or two later ate a humble meal on the ground with a family who had called him to chant over one of them. This was life so far, moving back and forth between two extreme points.

His father had given him flashing obsidian eyes and blue-black hair, now waist-length. He usually dressed for comfort working around two or three homesteads, or in dressier western garb men selected nowadays when called upon to visit or be employed away from home. More often than not he chose highly polished pointed-toe boots with a thick heel making him a wee bit taller, but was just as at ease in moccasins he patterned and made himself. He paired the latter with a bright scarf tied around his head when he conducted ceremonies.

Today he was in a western cut suit with a tan Stetson. His hair was in a long ponytail. As soon as he arrived home, he began to change his clothing. First, the hat landed on a peg. Then he sat down to slowly pull off his boots, each clunking heavily on the wood floor. He lifted a bulky turquoise bolo tie over his head, then unsnapped the dark blue shirt as he turned and saw himself in the bedroom mirror, giving a nod.

I dreamed this... Me, standing here...

He was over fifty years old; everyone said he looked a decade younger.

A side of him was too serious, showing up often in his attitude toward life when he spoke to his children and grandchildren. To his credit, he wasn't always so. A practical joker, too, he loved playing tricks on his brothers and sisters.

Right now, midafternoon, he was a bit off being his usual self after driving five hours, and sitting on a plane all morning.

"How's the big city?" Lily asked in their language, as she appeared at the bedroom door.

Austin wrinkled his brows, "Always the same. Me, I'm exhausted."

He dug into a small bag, pulled out a shiny gift-wrapped box and switched to English. "With love," he said flatly, speaking very tenderly and cutting the last word short. He handed the box over. Then he winked.

"Where's everyone?"

Their house sat a short distance from her parents' house. There were no near neighbors. When he drove up, both houses were quiet. Dogs and cats met him.

She slid lavender ribbons off the tiny silver box while he lay back on the bed and then she went to the kitchen.

She raised her voice from there. "Parents went to town. Eric went over to your folks. Are you hungry?"

He was quiet until she appeared again.

Shirtless, he handed his belt to her.

He didn't mean to sleep. Closing his eyes, pictures of New York City formed until images of his family superimposed those of the city.

His body jumped involuntarily, waking him.

My experiences here and far are such contrasts to each other... Take yesterday...

He looked up at the familiar ceiling and the light fixture. They reassured him and he closed his eyes again.

Yesterday he visited a large art museum to see an Egyptian show receiving rave reviews in the papers and on television. As soon as he entered the first wing he nearly stumbled over a display encased in low acrylic boxes. Semi-darkness affected everyone's vision; a security guard raced forward. He felt large and clumsy.

He didn't stay long. Painted lapis eyes in a frozen alabaster face followed him across the room. Eventually though he decided they weren't as threatening as the eyes of the security guard staring at him over a stone sarcophagus. Austin went to the only reasonably lit area in the building until his vision adjusted, a spray of lights aimed at a carved face reflecting a high burnish. Then he made a hasty exit.

Outside the building he sunk down on concrete steps to wait for others. The few designated places to sit were claimed and the flow of pedestrians was heavy, not quite frantic though rush hour was almost upon them. Working people were brusque. Tourists moved more leisurely, with time to spare.

He moved out of the way to a spot along the lower wall of the building where a few visitors rested. Leaning his head against its coolness, he placed the Stetson on his lap. The sun on his face made him drowsy.

Cars honked occasionally; a whir of voices hovered around him.

Whirlwinds...

He once lived in a place like this on the west coast. At the time it suited him, his youth and curious nature.

"Excuse me." A woman's voice interrupted. He angled himself away, closer to the cool wall.

"Um, excuse me. You there! Excuse me!"

She blocked the sun, towering over him as she did. He couldn't see her clearly until his eyes adjusted. A long tie-dyed skirt and a billowing blouse of gauze allowed sun light to pour right through them. He thought of the full-bodied women in the museum paintings caught in ornate frames of gold.

Heavy legs and large breasts were clearly outlined. She carried a square denim bag with embroidered floral designs. When she stepped forward, her hips were nearly eye level to him. She was looking down at him with saucer-sized eyes. They might have been more enticing in another place and time. A long strand of light brown hair blew into her mouth as she spoke and she pulled it away.

"Are you Indian?" Her voice was girlish, much younger than her age.

He nodded.

I've been there so many times...

"Would you mind if I sit?" She moved close, leaning over him. A loose breast swung toward him like a heavy bowling ball. He unconsciously moved his head out of the way, to one side.

He shook his head no and rubbed his eyes.

"May I sit?" She didn't wait to settle down in front of him. The thin skirt whirled around her and covered one of his boots. He rearranged himself.

She introduced herself in a bubbly, chatty way.

Five minutes later he didn't remember her name.

Once she started talking, she wouldn't, or couldn't, stop. He put his hat on the cement between them, and leaned against the wall again.

"Your people were true free spirits. Don't you agree? I've tried to live free like that, too."

Around them, glinting metal ants stalled in the streets.

"What kind of Indian are you?"

"Navajo," he replied without looking at her.

"Are you really? You look like Sioux."

She was thoughtful for a minute. "I'd like to learn to speak Sioux someday. When there's time. I heard that that language is dying out. Maybe I can help save it." She smiled cheerily at him. He nodded and it encouraged her.

She stretched out her legs. The metal on her sandals made little scraping noises on the cement.

"Where do you come from?" she asked.

"Arizona."

Most of the conversation was memorized. It was common coast to coast.

It was bound to come...

"Do you know any shamans?"

He pursed his lips, frowned, shaking his head no.

"Not too long ago, I met one right here! We got along all right, too. He asked me to come to his place. Said he'd show me a thing or two."

Blue eyes were piercing.

"Well, I went because I didn't want to pass up an opportunity like that. When I got there, he said that in order for him to teach me anything, I had to sleep with him first."

Austin wasn't sure if she was joking or serious.

She may have read his face and quieted for the first time. He studied her, the dropped shoulders, the downturn of her mouth, and the brushing away of some small thing on her skirt.

"It wasn't too bad," she confessed with a wrinkled forehead. "But I didn't learn very much. Later he said he had to go home and get approval for what he was going to teach me. He said he was the youngest shaman among his people. He was twenty-six, and even though he had lived in the city all his life, had been trained for this work since he was a kid."

"Where is he?" He asked, mildly interested.

"He went home a few weeks ago. I expected him back by now," she said, her voice rising.

Same story... Everywhere...

"No shamans?" she asked again pointblank.

He closed his eyes. "No," he lied, "They're all gone now."

"Do you know anybody who'd be willing to help me?" she asked insistently, leaning against his shoulder. A breast brushed the fold of his arm.

"Help you do what?"

She backed away and quieted.

After a while she stood and said, "Well, it was great meeting you." Hesitating, she studied him and tried again. "If you don't know anyone here, I'd be glad to show you around." She thrust a hip at him. Sunlight radiated through the skirt.

"I'm doing okay," he said.

Her sandals stepped away.

That was yesterday...

He heard his own soft snore and gave into it completely. He was home now and those encounters were far away.

Home... Family...

He slept deeply then heard Lily in the kitchen. The aroma of fresh coffee woke him and he got up. She was wiping coffee grinds off the stove top. The pot had boiled over and she was muttering to herself. A sewing machine was temporarily placed on the kitchen table where she had been working. He stepped up quietly behind her, catching her; his arms encircled her waist. Then he gently turned her around, brushing long hair back from her face to examine small diamond earrings. She wouldn't look at him, stepped away, and was quickly out of reach.

"Diamonds! Diamonds!" he said and whistled. "Lily, do they make you forget about dirt roads, lost kids and poor old folks? I almost forgot when the money went to them instead of necessities here."

"Tiny diamonds," Lily responded.

"Tiny diamonds then."

He returned to the bedroom to put on a shirt. When he came back, a sandwich was on the table and Lily sat on the other side.

"Thanks for the earrings, Austin. They cost way too much I'm sure."

"Well, you can give them to one of the girls if they don't please you."

Pouring a cup of coffee he asked, "Now, what's been going on while I've been away?"

It was Lily's turn to pour coffee while telling him about the cattle first, "Eric found two of them on Purple Mesa. I don't know why they went over there. He's looking for another one today. He's riding one of your father's horses.

I think he's hoping his grandpa will give him that one. His heart is set on it."

"Well, if his grandpa doesn't, he should buy one himself," Austin responded. "That's what a man does."

Then Lily listed each message left for him and told him about other events that occurred. She was reserved, business like, not her usual warm self. It was in her tone and posture.

Something's off...

"I made a contribution to one of my relatives for funeral expenses."

He expressed surprise and sympathy.

"Is there more?" he asked when Lily finished talking. "If not, I'd like to go visit my mother and father and find out what's happening with Dusty."

"There *is* something," Lily said setting her cup down and staring directly at him. She folded her arms.

"What?"

"Your daughter visited," she said slowly, restraining herself.

"Debra? Maggie? Did the grandchildren come too? They should visit more often."

"Neither of them. It was your *other* daughter."

He was puzzled. "Yeah?" he asked, "What's the joke?" He was about to get up and leave.

"It's no joke, Austin. She was here and she's coming back to see you this evening or tomorrow."

Clearly, Lily was upset.

He frowned and repeated, "My other daughter?"

"From California," Lily added.

"My other daughter—from California?" he asked stupidly.

What?

"Yes, Austin! Her mother is Mona!" Lily said emphasizing the name.

"Oh, you mean Ramona! Mona has a child? How old is she?" He was completely surprised.

"About thirty, I guess. She could be younger. She looks like a little girl under the make-up she wears. Her name is Melanie. Austin, why didn't you tell me? All those years and you never said anything!" She was growling and throwing up her arms.

"Why?"

"I didn't know," he answered calmly. "I didn't know."

It was all so unexpected. He didn't have any words.

Ramona... A lifetime ago...

He and Lily turned away from each other.

Finally, she said, "Well, I spoke to your mother and father about her. They know she's here to find you."

He was still speechless but nodded.

"There's something else. Her mother died recently."

He stayed quiet, thinking.

"Too bad. She was a good person," he said to himself more than Lily. "We just weren't meant for each other."

"Then Melanie *is* your daughter?" Lily was nearly shouting.

"I don't know. She could be I guess. Mona wasn't carrying a child that I knew of when she left here. I'm almost sure. I just don't know."

He turned toward the window remembering the day Mona left over. What else could he say about this new development?

Lily cleaned the table, put things away in an orderly manner.

He asked, "Shall we go?" then went out the door.

They made the five mile drive and as they drove up, saw Eric at the corral. Austin honked and waved. Hunter's truck was parked at Curtis's place.

Four little children played outside. Austin picked up each one and swung them around in the air; the toddling girls giggled and tried to run from him.

The two of them sat down across from his mother and father. They talked about New York City first and then the cattle. Eric, Hunter, and Curtis joined them.

His father finally said, "The ceremony for Dusty will be this weekend. All the family know. Some will be unable to come. That's all right. Now, we must decide how we want it to proceed."

They talked for nearly another hour before everyone turned to him He said uncertainly, "I guess you know something has happened. While I was away this week, a young woman visited. She claims I'm her father. I'm at a loss to explain it right now."

Hunter and Curtis gently teased him about his loss of memory. He saw Eric watching Lily.

Then Hunter warned, "Brother, if this is your daughter, she must be treated like one."

Austin's father just listened. His mother held her tongue, too.

Fatherhood... Manhood...

↑↑↑

Something new lay in the clear evening, something not detected before. He was looking out the window toward disappearing light, searching. He always tried to see ahead as best he could and here he had fallen short.

A barely audible knock interrupted his thoughts. There was a flurry of steps and Lily led Melanie inside.

Austin turned around and met her, extending a hand. She took it and he held her hand loosely. They stood rather awkwardly, facing each other. She stared at him as if she didn't quite believe it was him. He returned his own puzzled gaze.

I see Ramona... Another Ramona...

"Lily, please come here."

He grasped Lily's hand in his free one and he stood between the two women, loosely holding onto both of them. He had jumped right into it, though it wasn't his way. He was still his father's son.

"Melanie, I'm Austin. Lily tells me that you've been looking for me." He squeezed Lily's hand, and then let go of both women.

"Let's sit," suggested Lily.

When they settled down, he said encouragingly, "You've something more to tell us?"

A strange beginning... But we must start somewhere...

Melanie took a deep breath and moved her mouth. No words came out. This was uneasy for her too.

She told of her mother's death first, then her stepfather's passing, and life in Los Angeles. She paused, uncertain what to add.

They visited about two hours but Austin still hadn't responded to her claim that she was his daughter. It was getting dark; she was preparing to drive back to town.

"It's time now," Melanie said. "I hope I don't get lost. The last time I came out, I took a wrong turn."

Let her stay or go?

When she rose, Austin and Lilly did too. Another awkward pause came. Then he said slowly, thinking his words through, "Melanie, I didn't know your mother was expecting a child when she left here. If I would have known, our lives may have been different."

He looked at Lily and said, "After your mother left, I went on with my life and made another family. This is my wife now and we have children and grandchildren. I'm loyal to them. But if you say you're my daughter, I guess I and my family must accept that claim."

He embraced Melanie while looking at Lily over Melanie's shoulder. Lily's eyes met his.

Then he walked Melanie to her car.

When he returned, he sat down beside Lily and let out a long breath. She said in a low voice, "Austin, you're one of a kind." He heard a small sigh.

What choice is here but to make the best of what comes...

Dusty

DUSTY WAS BORN in the 1930s. That's all he knew. That little cloud of uncertainty about the exact year made two furrows deepen on his forehead whenever age came up; otherwise his mother's story rang true.

She said...

"Your father broke a black stallion the day you were born and he came inside thirsty and tired It was dusty that day; the stallion was part wind, whirling in circles until it spun him off. He lay there testing his bones to see if he was whole before picking himself up. Then he brushed dirt and hay off his hat and clothes. As soon as he entered the house, I put you in his sore arms. He didn't tell about his tumble until later.

"He admired you. When he gave you back to me, his dusty prints were all over you.

"Before going out to face the stallion again, he asked, 'Do you want to be the first to ride this wild horse, my baby?'"

That's what she remembered... Not the exact year... Not the day...

Dusty was the sixth one; times were tough, days stretched out like barbed wire. The family labored sunrise to sunset just to hang on. All were wispy thin; a blustery wind might knock over any of them. The skimpiest times, when they lived solely on two foods, luckily, were few.

In the same red and purple valley where his mother and father were born, he too crawled about and later toddled after Hunter, Mary, Sammy, Wayne and Austin. Hunter was eagerly going into his teens and Sammy was about ten years older than Dusty.

Between the ages of one to three, he rode on Hunter's shoulders. From up there he eyed the bigger world. In stinging hot sand and rare crunchy snow, the two of them took the sheep out daily and kept each other company.

I felt safe then... Peace was everywhere... From the sun down to ground and upward again...

Under glances of nearby grown-ups, he joined his brothers in their work when he and Hunter weren't trailing bleating sheep. He favored spring when the family dug earth in a warm burst of energy and everyone stayed outside all the time. Even though he did it lazily and like the baby he was, he dropped seeds, too, and behind him, someone came along covering them. At night he sat, stood, or walked on hot aching backs and knew for himself, for the first time, how a man's body might refuse to bend and give any more, but in the faintness of next sunrise everyone leaned into the furrows again. Yes, his family got by, and looking back, it hadn't been too bad. Much of it was fun.

At the age of eight or nine, two men drove from the nearest town and he overheard one tell his father, "We're looking for children, those not too old and too little. We want them to go to school. They'll eat well over there and learn a new way."

Tiny lines appeared on his father's face as he gave it thought, and with Susie's agreement, he beckoned four of them. They stood looking at their mother and father curiously. Then their curiosity quickly became excitement, mixed with heaviness. That very same afternoon, Wayne, Austin, Dusty and Richard were signed up, and unexpectedly found themselves riding in a car to boarding school.

There wasn't much to take. Their clothes were packed in a flat, oblong cardboard box to be sorted out later, but those few possessions may just as well have stayed behind.

The visiting grownups rushed to put the boys in the backseat of the car, maybe the first his father was able to inspect close up. It happened so fast there was no time to enjoy that first ride in a chugging vehicle or for emotional outbursts. That came later for Dusty.

Looking back, I ask why the hurry? Hurry… Hurry…

School was new, squeezed onto four acres. The night they arrived they all stayed in the same room; it smelled strange and sounded hollow. Wayne took charge and told them where to sleep and he nudged them awake the next morning. Then a handful of his people acting as interpreters called them, one by one, into a line. Each returned with a nearly bald head; long hair lay in heaps on the floor. That was followed by hot baths and then they were told to slip into a set of new clothes and tight new shoes. The shaved heads emphasized their cranial bones, the dips and lumps there, their luminous eyes and gawky uncoordinated bodies.

They studied each other afterward careful to hide their thoughts, but Dusty secretly saw a softness that had been exposed in them, especially in him and Richard; he wanted to shield it.

They were unable to fully understand all the instructions given the first two weeks. Half a dozen teachers, not of their people, taught everyone. Because of that, children and teachers didn't communicate very well. The youngest children couldn't conceal their fear and loneliness.

Me and Richard cried to go home, but Wayne and Austin showed no emotion.... Later I was able to have no feelings at all...

That place was different; it sat apart from life and discipline they knew. Though not far from home the youngest two didn't know others when they arrived. For the first time, they slept on beds every night and ate new foods which were filling but unsatisfying. Dusty and Richard were put in the same grade but couldn't understand anything their teacher said and she didn't understand them either. Both sides wore confused faces when they looked at each other.

Her name was Miss Finch, a tall young woman with unruly locks of sandy colored hair that fell into her eyes when she taught class and she looked at them through the straw. First she wanted them to speak English. Every morning the class repeated "Good morning, Miss Finch" a dozen times, or until she was satisfied. Dusty and Richard had no idea what they were saying or doing until Wayne explained what Miss Finch expected.

When the boys left their mother and father, none of them knew four full months would pass before they came together again. That long first separation was anxious. Even with luxuries of abundant food, bed, shelter and new shoes, he and Richard continued to miss their mother and father, but it was especially true for Richard. In the meantime, they learned abc's and managed to say, "Good morning, Miss Finch," well enough, though they clipped words and changed the sounds.

Goot Moan, Miss Fence...

Dusty and Richard stuck together most of the time while Wayne and Austin joined an older group. Outside class, dorm attendants caught all the boys in their care and led them to their assigned chores, or talked sternly to them when there were fights.

On Sundays everyone was taken to church.

First time was scary.... The leader was mad... He made his voice really big and flapped his arms... Sounded mean to us...

Thanksgiving and Christmas were mentioned for the first time. All they really grasped at their early ages and in the new language was that those days were to eat. That part they truly enjoyed.

Four months later, their father arrived and happily they left with him.

At home their extended family looked at them with bemused expressions, taking in and lingering on the shaved heads. When the boys told all the things they were doing in school, their mother seemed to look deep inside them and she shifted her mouth around, but didn't utter approval or disapproval.

Following sheep in the crusty snow of January, Dusty and Richard announced matter-of-factly to their parents, "We don't want to go back." Wayne and Austin, however, looked forward to it. The four returned and settled into a pattern that didn't alter while they were there. Their long stay was broken up by short breaks at home.

After a year, Miss Finch was replaced by a much older and more formal woman who showed no patience whatsoever with broken English. Miss Oswald. She cringed each time they mispronounced words, covering her ears. She whacked them soundly on the back or stretched their lips mercilessly about in the air, trying to force their mouths to form words and sounds she wanted. Actually, at that time, he and Richard were still mimicking sounds. Full meaning evaded them. Miss Oswald complained, "You're speaking too much trash, to the detriment of English."

Trash... Detrimen'... What's that?

She stood in front of school officials stubbornly, bringing along some children and pointing accusingly at them. Punishment for speaking their own language was the rule during Miss Oswald's reign. Dusty had his mouth washed out with soap for breaking that rule on three occasions. For years, the taste of soap scum welled up in his mouth now and then.

Richard, because he was youngest, split from Dusty and went with a younger group. He wanted to be more cooperative than Dusty with Miss Oswald. Her wrath was painful. When Richard voiced this, Dusty laughed but knew exactly what he meant.

Miss Oswald was a giant, standing just under six feet with muscles of steel. She wrestled the boys when necessary and forced soap into their mouths herself as in one instance with Dusty. Her hands gripped Dusty firmly, snapped his limber body this way and that, and he quickly gave in, all his toughness breaking down in her steely grip.

I wanted to kill her...

Neither did she tolerate hair, especially longer hair, often sending boys back to dorm attendants to shave their heads more closely. Furthermore, she closely inspected everyone's ears. Even the oldest students put up with the humiliation and tender earlobes after she jerked them towards her to look inside. The oldest students didn't worry about soap; they were rapped bluntly on the hands with rulers and other instruments. Flesh and bone stung. Stung.

Dusty stayed seven years mastering the basics of English, though all his life he lapsed into a broken form of it and, later on, into a kind of broken Navajo. Miss Oswald said to him on the day of their parting, "It's been my greatest challenge to teach you anything—let alone English."

He narrowed his eyes at her, trying to make his face as scornful as he could, and she returned his effort with a deathly coldness that sent shivers down his spine. He was about fifteen at the time and she, perhaps, in her fifties. It was hard to guess the age of old people.

I wanted to kill her...

By the time he and Miss Oswald went separate ways, he had some weight, was of medium height with a trim build, and putting aside the boarding school haircut, Dusty stood out in any crowd.

He learned two things very well in school but they weren't habits the teachers desired or things his family at home knew.

When I was about thirteen I took my first drink... Some older boys brought it, passed it around... Two bottles...

It happened on a weekend. His group met in a screen of trees behind the dorm. One of them, nicknamed Sidewinder, held the bottle up to Dusty and ordered, "Drink!" Dusty inhaled its strong odor and made a face, wrinkling his nose and curling up a corner of his mouth.

He took the bottle anyway, swirled the liquid around and tilted the bottle up. All the others, about seven of them, cheered and hit Dusty on the back in a congratulatory slap as Dusty choked on the burn. He smelled his own whiskey breath.

A warm flush coursed through his body and he stood back while others took their turn. It affected all of them the same; they experienced a wondrous and powerful mood for a brief time. Toward the end of the bottle, Dusty heard himself call Sidewinder, "Siderider," and "Winesider," and Sidewinder didn't notice because he was too caught up in everything else that was happening. Then feeling very brave, the group lapsed into some forbidden Navajo phrases and words.

We were crazy... Our words were so fuzzy...

The group laughed recklessly, trying to make sense of what they were saying and doing. One by one they fell onto the sand. Pow. Pow.

Toward nightfall, Wayne came looking for him. Everyone, with the exception of Sidewinder, lay sprawled out.

Later Wayne told him, "Sidewinder sat right there with a sly smile, watching all of you. I don't trust him."

Dusty lay face up and Wayne shook him. Dusty growled back; Sidewinder chuckled and taunted, "Want some more?"

Something in me turned right then...

School was harder afterward.

Because Dusty and Sidewinder were older than the others, they were more severely disciplined.

Wayne finished school such as it was and left. He had been the boys' real leader, not dorm attendants or school officials. He was their refuge in the first of those years, comforting them when they didn't know what to expect and counseling them when they needed it. On their own, the world was too big, too demanding.

Give in, it said...

That was drilled into them in class and by aides in the dorm. With Wayne no longer there to remind them of their mother's and father's presence and to make sense of their experiences, Dusty and Richard came to a crossroad.

Austin left next, right after Wayne, and Richard became ill enough to go home, about the same time Austin left. Dusty was alone.

That didn't bother me... I could take care of myself...

11

What made school fun was girls…

He was very appealing until they got to know him.

The real me…

By then, Dusty felt his emotions taking over. Their force built up big and then subsided, back and forth. Back and forth.

Close to turning sixteen or seventeen, ready to go out on his own, two ominous things happened.

To school came a young woman who wanted little use of English, and some other things it offered, and she was from the same place as Dusty.

She was there only two weeks.

The last time he saw her, she was a little girl, but Deezbaah had grown into quite a young woman. Her long glistening hair was tied back with yarn and she wore a long skirt when he first saw her at school. They immediately recognized each other.

Remarkably, when she was called to have her hair shorn, she shook her head "no" and stepped back from the attendants. Her simple disagreement signaled trouble.

Next, when new clothes were issued, she just stood there, staring at them. She didn't pick them up at all. Those incidents were the talk of the school.

To top everything off, she spoke her own language often, in clear violation of school rules.

About a week after her arrival, she disagreed with aides when she wanted to leave for an hour without earlier permission. Family members stood by but were not permitted to take her off school grounds just then.

When they departed, in the quiet office the aides and officials told her, "You won't go to the next meal." Deezbaah left that room, but a matron followed.

"You're sulking," the matron told her, "and you know our rules. Stay in your room the rest of the day, and in the morning you can pick up the regular schedule." Left alone, she wandered about outside the dorm until the same matron led her to a smaller room than her own in the building and turned a key in the door.

When Deezbaah was finally released, her depression was seen by other students.

Several stood outside the detention room when the door was unlocked. She came out hesitantly. Seeing Dusty's face in a small crowd of the curious, she approached him and told her story.

"This place is like a deep canyon that's hard to escape," she said in their language. "I wish I didn't come here."

She didn't get sympathy from Dusty. He answered, "Just give in."

"No," she responded. "No!"

"Who do you think you are?" Dusty asked pointedly.

Deezbaah looked crushed and rushed away.

The next day, a school day, Sidewinder came around, with three others. He was still there. He was almost as old as Austin but his progress was slower. He brought something along, a dark brown bottle and he handed it to Dusty.

Their crowd was restless; their energy was dark, threatening as deep choppy water. The boys walked toward the girls' dorm. In the distance Deezbaah came from the cafeteria. Day was becoming darker. All the lines of the buildings around them were murky.

"Hey look!" Sidewinder said, pointing to Deezbaah. "That girl makes me sick!" He mimicked the gliding way she walked.

Dusty watched her cross the ground and agreed, "Yeah, me too."

"Hey, Dusty, she knows you. Bring her over here," Sidewinder ordered.

His tone made Dusty cautious and he refused, "Nah."

Sidewinder pushed him and all the other boys backed him up, "Go get her."

Dusty gave in and went toward Deezbaah. She saw him and waited.

"What you doing?" he asked, looking behind him. Sidewinder and the others were still visible in evening light.

"Working late," Deezbah said in their language. And in English she said, "I'm punished."

"Let's go for a walk," Dusty said, taking her hand. She didn't pull away; she went along as Dusty walked toward Sidewinder. Halfway there he saw that she smelled him and felt her soft hand try to pull away.

She stopped and planted her feet there. Then Sidewinder and the others started coming toward them. Dusty reassured her. "Don't be afraid," he said.

She calmed herself and let him hold her hand a minute longer.

Sidewinder came up and grabbed Deezbah around the waist. He was smellier than Dusty and she was immediately frightened again.

"Let me go," she said in Navajo.

"Speak English!" Sidewinder said. "We speak English here!"

The other members of the group surrounded them while Sidewinder ran his hand down the front of Deezbaah's blouse. Terrified, she yelled, "Dusty!"

He simply turned, pushed the others back and walked away.

It was easy to do that... It's powerful to have no feeling...

When he looked back, the others were tugging at

Deezbaah's blouse. Still he had no reaction. He knew this girl, he thought. He knew her a long time.

Deezbaah screamed. She pushed the boys back, reaching out, flinging her arms, trying to strike them. He heard his name again and he looked back. Her blouse was partly ripped.

The screen door at the cafeteria opened.

Someone stood there. "What are you boys doing?" A man in the doorway began walking toward them.

Dusty went back and said calmly, "That's enough. Leave her alone."

Sidewinder didn't want to let her go, shoving his face in front of Dusty's. He met Sidewinder's ugly sneer. The rest of the group waited to see if Sidewinder was going to take it.

"Whore," he spit.

First time I heard that kind of word...

Deezbaah pulled her blouse together. Tears rolled down her face. The man from the cafeteria approached.

Sidewinder and the others quickly ran. After they left, Deezbah became hysterical and shouted at Dusty, "Why'd you let them do that?"

"Nothing happened," Dusty said. "They didn't hurt you. Besides it's your fault, acting the way you do."

Deezbaah yelled, "I thought you were my relative. My family said we're related. Is this the way to treat each other?" She stepped back from him; he stepped forward.

The man who came up, a large man, grabbed Dusty by a bicep and said, "Wait a minute!"

"Everything's all right."

The man loosened his grip but didn't let go.

He heard it all. He heard Dusty answer, "Not here... We're not related over here." He laughed loudly at his joke, trying to grab Deezbaah and kiss her lips. He felt himself yanked back roughly and this time the man held him fiercely. Dusty hung in the man's iron hand.

Pure disgust crossed Deezbaah's face. Even in Dusty's daze, he too had shock. He felt uneasy. She was so angry.

The man pulled Dusty into glaring light, looking him in the eye. He grabbed Dusty's arms, twisted one behind his back, and told Deezbaah to leave.

Dusty never saw her after that. When he came to his senses he had remorse and Deezbaah's look of horror stayed with him a few weeks before he was able to shake it off.

What I remember is Sidewinder touching her... Me with no wish to help her... I had no feeling...

In the intervening years, he'd seen her a couple of times from afar. He recognized her but made sure to keep his distance.

The other thing happened a few days after she left.

Sidewinder was with Dusty again They were with others and all had passed a silly lightheartedness and moved on to anger, after a couple of drinks. They were like dangerous, caged, animals finally let loose. Dusty and Sidewinder left school and their group to go to a place near the river where Sidewinder looked for a bootlegger. On their way back, with his prize tucked inside Sidewinder's pant leg, they came across an old man sitting peacefully under a tree. He nursed a bottle of his own with no attempt to conceal it. He was perhaps sixty.

The man was clearly one of them, but he surprised Dusty and Sidewinder by saying in English, "Go on kids. Go play."

They burst into laughter. The man, feeling no pain, laughed with them, exposing missing teeth. The three of them talked a bit and the man looked in the direction of the school nearby.

"Go school," he said. "It's pretty good I think. You smarter than me."

"What do *you* know, you old thing?" Dusty heard himself say.

"Know nothing," the man replied. "Told you, not smart. You kids, you smart."

"Where'd you learn English?" asked Sidewinder.

"I teach me," said the man with his toothless grin.

Sidewinder asked him abruptly, "Do you have money?"

The man grinned again and said, "None."

Sidewinder asked another question, "You have another bottle?"

The man chuckled and shook his head no, "No money. No bottle."

"This one will do," Sidewinder said, yanking it away.

He took a drink while the man squinted up at him and said slowly, "Maybe... Maybe... Maybe kids not smart." Sidewinder shoved the bottle at Dusty.

"What do you mean?" Dusty asked.

"I'm old," the man said. "Kids not old."

"Hey, what's that mean?" Dusty asked after taking another swig.

The man made a wide mocking grin and asked, "You want be old?"

Dusty glared at him and shook his head. "Like you? No!" He spit his words.

Sidewinder was impatient, too. He answered, lifting the old man's bottle again, "No, we don't want to be old. We're kids, remember? We want to have fun."

"Old not for kids," the man said. "Old, hard!"

"Shut up!" Sidewinder said. "I'm tired of you!"

At Sidewinder's tone, the man started to get up. His grin was gone.

He had a pouch the boys hadn't noticed until he stood and it stuck out of his jacket pocket.

"Trying to hold out on us?" Sidewinder said, jerking the pouch, before the man could grab it. Sidewinder tore it open and discovered little bags of powders, arrowheads, and feathers. Dusty knew what the pouch was, but Sidewinder didn't. Sidewinder scattered everything into the air.

The man tried to grab all the items falling to the ground, but Sidewinder pushed him aside. He landed hard and Sidewinder kicked him lightly in the stomach. Still, it knocked the wind from him.

Before they left, Dusty stood over the man and said, "Those things no good. They don't help."

The man lay there, holding his belly. He said very quietly, "You kids not be old."

His comment was unsettling and in the silence after it, Dusty heard a gurgle nearby, the river; the tree branches overhead squeaked and swayed.

"Who cares?" Dusty said, watching him try to sit up and breathe normally.

"Your mother..." answered the old man, tapping his chest, "Your kids..."

"You're crazy!" Dusty said. He put a shoe on the old man's belly and held him down. His meanness was rising up.

I felt his eyes on my back when I walked away...

☨☨☨

School was over... I headed out... Far from home... The farther the better...

He went to Albuquerque to work in late spring. Richard had come back to school after a few months' absence and wanted to stay there another year. He told Dusty, "I'll be there later. I'll follow."

A couple of seasons whisked by and Dusty knew he was barely making it. That's why he decided to move in with a young woman, Carmen, and her family. From them he picked up his meager Spanish. Her mother and father owned a tiny plot of land along the Rio Grande. In many ways they lived like his people because they were very poor and did almost all the same things to make ends meet, existing only on coffee and tortillas when they had to.

Carmen was warm, intense, lively. Black eyes and raven colored hair made her very attractive but her full body was what he first wanted. She was older by three years. After he really got to know Carmen, he discovered her soft, gigantic heart. She was very kind, treating him far better than he deserved, taking him in when he had no money and job, and putting him in her bed and keeping him warm. She was the first woman he showed genuine affection, and for nearly two years, she and her family's place were comforting and fulfilling.

Then one night, his hands, racing over her soft smooth body, detected a change in her flat belly. For a couple of weeks he traced that burgeoning spot, and each time, felt a quickening under his fingers. "Carmen," he asked, "What's this?" She sat up in bed, a silky shadow, and then stood, motioning him to follow. In the tiny sky-blue kitchen with a lamp flicking hypnotically, she told him of their coming child and said, deliriously happy, "Dusty, honey, our baby will be called Angel if it is a girl and Jesus if it is a boy." Her voice was high and musical.

She was excited, breathless. Her face and body were velvety in that light and she looked like an angel herself, sitting in the darkened kitchen, daring to share her dream. "Our baby, he or she, will grow up to be Governor, or the Governor's wife, and, of course, will be so handsome or beautiful that anyone who looks upon him or her will fall under a spell." High pitched laughter filled the tiny room like splashing water.

Dusty gulped. Could anyone like that come from his flawed and mortal self?

"I'm going out to celebrate," he told her the next day. He left the house and woke up in Tucson three days later. He never looked back.

Again, I felt power in just walking away...

Richard caught a ride to Tucson to spend some time with him. From there they went north to Phoenix to a string of sickly-sweet-smelling women. Dusty fixed Richard up several times because his brother wasn't the go-getter he was, but the girls and women he picked were always older, with a hard edge on them. They didn't match Richard. When Dusty offered his own young woman, the one on his arm, Richard stumbled backward in shock. She, clinging to Dusty's arm, purred until Richard replied, "No," and then she hissed, squinting marble eyes at him.

Brawls started wherever Dusty was; he never walked away from one. In fact he was at the center. Amazingly he always emerged the victor in all those tangles.

A part of me loved it...

He felt Richard's uneasiness the whole time with this way of living but they never talked about it.

They moved on to Salt Lake and Denver in a continuing blur of fights and women. Richard fell into a somber and searching mood.

Finally he came and said, "Brother, I'm going back. I'm going home."

Dusty stared at him but kind of knew it would end like that.

"How 'bout you?" Richard dared to ask.

"There's nothing over there, miles of it..."

"Go with me," Richard urged.

"No, no," Dusty shook his head, pulling out some crumpled bills from his shirt pocket and transferring them to Richard's shirt pocket.

Dusty went on like that up to his enlistment.

Then I hitchhiked home to tell what I'd done... Joined up....

His mother met him at the door, opening her arms. A soft shoulder braced him. She looked a lot more worn when he had the chance to really study her. His father also grabbed him the way he did when Dusty was a child. Briefly, he was tempted to feel something, or feel more deeply than usual, as he observed his parents this time around, but what would that do?

Off he went to Korea!

All I remember is sitting in hillsides, staring off into space, waiting... Waiting...

He came back in one piece with a small wound in his shoulder. Afterward whenever he had the chance, he took to pulling off that side of his shirt to show off the scar.

His father suggested a couple of healing ceremonies to counter war ways, but Dusty didn't show when his father wanted to talk about those plans.

I just walked away...

IV

Seasons turned... Luck changed...

Instead of winning, now it went the other way. Dusty

was a loser; opponents whipped him soundly, over and over, yet he couldn't let go of them.

He called no one friend or brother; he was always alone.

Women were still interested until he spoke his mind; then they packed their bags and flew.

His body reflected the tumbles he had. Good looks, physical strength, were slipping away while his mind filled with flitting things that never settled but could never be clearly seen. He roamed restlessly.

On occasion, he found himself standing where the old school once was, now sun-bleached structures boarded up and partly falling down.

Empty like me...

More than once, he found himself down by the river where the old man asked, "You want be old?"

He laughed out loud at the memory but it was without joy, just a sound, a grimace.

He didn't go home anymore because he was often too bruised and sore. He didn't want his mother and father to see him that way.

Skin and bones...

v

Hide... Run away...

Sometimes he didn't know where he was or what day it was; fog was his world. One day Wayne came hunting him and groped in the foggy layers, pulled on him.

"There's help, Dusty."

He forced himself to listen; fatigue, hunger, and every other little observation or sound easily pulled his attention away.

After Wayne left, he snickered at his brother's words.

I take care of Dusty...

But he wasn't able to pull it off. Finally he permitted himself to find the place Wayne mentioned. Arriving, he didn't want to enter there; stalling, he paused and looked upward, really looked. Winter hovered, close and clear. Giving into all this, he approached the double doors, glimpsing himself in the glass. Was that really him?

He turned and ran.

He went around the block, just moving to let go of an onslaught of resistant thoughts, until he arrived at the double doors again. The second time his reflection didn't scare him as before. Bitterly, he went inside, toward whatever destiny awaited him.

For a week or more, he lay in bed trying to withstand nightmares and a monstrous gnaw on him. To rise and look out the window was a trial. Then he surprised himself and agreed to move to a different place for longer care.

"I'll go," he said. "I'll go."

Shortly after that move, he woke one morning to a nurse who was sizing him up; he'd been yelling and thrashing his bedding.

"Mabel," she said as he settled down. "That's me."

Too self-absorbed to ever be nice to anyone, he told her outright, "Look, I hurt, but don't bother with me. I'm here just long enough to get on my feet and I'll be gone again."

He never cooperated with anyone.

"Why stay if you really don't want help?" she argued.

Too quickly he responded. "It's not for me... It's for my family..."

For my family!

What a liar he was!

"Leave," Mabel shot back, not at all fooled. "I'm no

doctor but it doesn't take one to see the way things are. It's not doing anybody any good if you're here against your will. There's the door." People passed in the hall.

She came into a bit more focus when she jutted her chin toward him. Hazel eyes. Full lips. A small scar below her left eye. He noticed slender hands and long fingers when she pushed her dark hair away from her face and turned quickly away. She was thin, almost skinny, with coppery skin.

Overwork aged her. Really, she was much younger than he guessed at that first meeting.

Gradually, day by day, they strategized how to put up with each other. Both studied the other over walls they put up. Eventually, they were able to stay in the same room together. Short spans of truce.

Her directness and no nonsense attitude were new for him and surprisingly, in his weakened state, he found a kind of peace in her firm care.

It had been forever that Carmen came to mind. Mabel brought those old days forward in little flashes. A flash of Carmen's face. A touch. A silky shadow.

From the rehabilitation center, Dusty went to Mabel's.

At that stage they called each other friend, promising to help each other out for a while, nothing more. He particularly repeated, "May, it's temporary. I don't stay anywhere long. I tell you when I'm on my feet, I'll be gone."

But numbed parts of me began to feel again...

VI

A happy dream...

Mabel already had two small daughters, Faith and Harmony. They were small and delicate. He gave in and smiled at their names. Kind of silly, he thought. It told him how really soft their mother was. When each little girl took him by a light little hand and led him inside the door, he was sure it was a strange, wondrous, and undeserving dream.

Often he found himself just sitting, observing, trying to absorb the three of them and his new situation. They left him alone and stayed on their side of the room. So, after years of chaos he'd come to this place of peace and acceptance.

Slowly, he turned around. Light flickered in his eyes, a tiny blaze; he laughed again. For the first time since Carmen, he had a woman who mattered to him.

When his father and mother met Mabel the first time in town, it was not planned. Dusty had a hand on Mabel's arm as they crossed the street. On the other side, his father and mother climbed out of Ross's truck. Up to that day, it was Dusty's practice to turn away or endure a hasty, uncomfortable, visit. Today he stopped, took a deep breath, and guided Mabel over. He put her in front of him and then stepped forward and told them who she was. His mother took her hand and nodded at her. His father did the same. Questions were in their eyes, but their conversation was not prying. A few minutes later, Faith and Harmony came running out of the store behind them. The girls were cheerful as they joined Mabel and Dusty. After Dusty introduced them, everyone parted. Dusty looked behind him and his father was still watching them.

Marriage came.

With a license and everything... Never did that before...

His body was on the mend. It wouldn't ever be what it was when he was young, but it was holding together. He worked steadily and he and Mabel were happy. Now and then, they made a trip to his mother and father's place.

Two more children came. A boy was born first, two years after their marriage.

"Let's call him Sammy," Dusty said, holding the new-born to his chest. Their daughter, Rena, followed about eighteen months later.

It was too good to last... That's what I say... Too good to last...

One rainy night on a dangerously slick road, he and Sammy drove to a nearby store to buy things for Dusty's lunch the next day. Dusty didn't see a dark truck creep along in front of him because it had no tail lights. When he finally saw it, he hit the brake too hard and fast, and all he remembered was an uncontrollable spin.

Pain... Crushing waves of pain...

Little Sammy left the world right then and Dusty cursed himself. For being out in the rain. For the rain itself. For not having better vision. For not having a better car. For everything.

Free of drinking the first years of his marriage, he went back to it again. It was the first thing he did in the morning and the last thing he did at night.

Mabel left him twice but allowed him back whenever he stopped.

On a recent anniversary of their little boy's death, Dusty confessed at the end of day, "May, I can't think of any reason to go on. You and the three girls should be enough for me. Try to forgive me when I tell you it's not.

"I've no strength to hang on."

Don't say it out loud, Dusty... No one wants to hear it...

"Some people call out to a god when they're down and out, but you know me. Have I ever been like that?"

Mabel looked forsaken. Part of him was beyond caring. Yet, he did feel something, a quiver in his throat and chest.

No one wants to hear you, Dusty... You're on your own...

PART FOUR

Shining Stream

Closing song

RECORDED BY KISH HAWKINS

Cody

H̶E STUDIED THE holy moon altar on the ground before him, the road of life pressed there, and felt a rippling surge in his heart, veins, and arteries propel him forward. Streams. New day.

It brings me here...

The tipi was full, in his care. Opaque sky floated above the smoke hole and earth supported him. Chirping birds hung over him.

All night he sat there, patiently holding his spine straight, folding his legs in such a way that he could stay like that until he completed the ceremony. Now it was time to release everyone.

His eyes went to the moon again, the road of life just beyond his black weathered boots.

I know well where this leads...

All the sacred things were put away; the ceremonial fire had ended, too. A small informal one twirled at the center of the tipi

He folded his arms leisurely, speaking in his usual direct way.

"This ceremony wants a few more words before we go out. For those who don't know... It's good to be reminded what we have gone through to have it." He looked at Dusty's daughters and then at others. His voice was hoarse and he cleared his throat.

Austin translated for Dusty's daughters and Mabel.

"This came from other tribes. They have their own stories about it...

"Some of us took to it right away though others didn't want anyone to use it. Some said this herb causes drunkenness and laziness. Some said men and women came in here to copulate with each other and animals, and to practice wife-swapping. Those are just a few of the things said about it."

His shoulders shook with a hint of silent laughter.

I never saw that... People being what we are, maybe it happened somewhere...

One of Dusty's daughter's mouth formed an O when Austin told them what was said.

Cody continued, "Some of us took it because it goes with what we know to be true. Laws of sky and earth. Their order. That guides us in here.

"When we leave, we don't go against teachings of the ceremony and we don't drink or use anything like that."

Some don't want to hear this... That this ceremony requires something from each of us...

A small ritual breakfast was going around the circle.

Cody unfolded his arms to stretch. He unfurled like a blade of grass in warm light.

"When we follow this road, we train ourselves. In here we sit up on the ground all night, trying not to slouch or to sleep. We stay inside, don't go out. We sacrifice comfort, sleep. We set our minds to accomplish difficult things to help ourselves and relatives.

"All of it is for that purpose."

Each day of life...

He stopped, rested his head on one shoulder and then on the other shoulder. A pop came from his neck.

"My relatives, really, our daily needs are few. It's enough to be on this land for a while and to be fully ourselves. An old man said that to me. You all know him. He was from here.

"In the face of fearful things, illness and hardships, we must go on, be content.

"This road is good for that."

He stopped speaking to take a spoonful of food from two bowls slowly making their way around the tipi. Then he waited for Austin to finish translating what he said.

I like to leave speeches to others... But now and then...

"There's a lot of confusion among us now.

"Some white people and Indians say the story of Peyote Woman, she who brought this herb, isn't true. They call it — fairy tale."

He said fairy tale in English, and it caused everyone to open their eyes wide and stare at him.

Fairy tale... Strange words... Hard to say...

He took a spoonful of food from another bowl and a couple of people said "fairy tale" jokingly while he passed the bowls on.

"We expect confusion from outsiders but not so much among our own people. Yet it happens.

"Some say believing in old times and old stories is our greatest downfall."

Our elders' stories... Truth is what they tell...

He gave Austin some time to speak and Austin made it short. Then he went on.

"Many of us fear ourselves today and any ancient knowledge still inside us. We try to cut that out of us, put it aside.

"Effects are all around. Some today, young and old alike, fear our healers and ceremonies. That's our grandmothers and grandfathers. They're the only ones who know those things."

He looked around the tipi, directly at each person. Took his time.

"Maybe a couple of us sitting in here now still don't quite trust medicine and this ceremony. Maybe we are thinking that way, too."

He turned to Dusty.

"Schools have a lot to do with it. Books, too. They want to convince us to stop being who we are. Stop learning the way we do."

The bowls moved to the last person in the circle. People waited to go out.

"My relatives, look around. Everywhere, people are searching for something to explain life. They want to find something holy.

"We have it. A holy way that makes sense for who we are. We have elders who help us, too. Divine nature helps us. These always guide us through, when the man-made world falls apart."

He nodded at Austin who summed up his words quickly.

"We all know this ceremony still has opposition. We accept that but we will defend it, too. We also know it's not for everyone. But for some of us it's just the thing."

Austin again put these last words into English, for the benefit of Dusty's daughters.

When the fireman opened the door, and Cody motioned all to go out, everyone stood and stretched. They had sat for nearly twelve hours straight.

When Cody came out he visited in the house and tipi

for a while. Then he sat outside alone in the breeze and let himself dissolve into it.

In the distance on life's edge, Chee walked slowly toward him, unsteady on his feet as ever.

Old timer...

Cody's own legs were also beginning to twist in their sockets and make dry little whispers to him. What it meant would become too clear too soon. It was a matter of cycling seasons, but he was prepared. For anything. For everything.

Now we become what was foretold...

Chee settled quietly beside him. They fell into silence. All had been said and done. What they had just finished was already gone—into air and light streams, forming something else again.

Faces of his grandchildren, great-grandchildren appeared in his mind.

Quanah...

Chee

*N*EVER ONE TO leap impetuously into any chasm when he was younger, it wasn't his behavior as a very old man. He felt his way, putting out a hand, guarding and leading his family. That preponderance always marked him. Yet he knew something else about himself. Something critical.

No one accomplishes anything in this world completely alone...

Right then he was rolling back events in the last couple of days, unrolling thoughts. The unexpected incident occurring yesterday with Dusty's daughter in the midst of everything else, so fearful! Leading Dusty into the tipi, no matter that his son was an aging man and no matter that he himself now had to creep carefully over the ground so he wouldn't shatter his dry bones and then had to cushion those brittle bones in soft thick sheepskins on the tipi ground! Him speaking to holy medicine and to divine nature on behalf of his offspring again! His wholehearted meditation through the night! Hunter and Austin helping him go outside in the middle of the ceremony! Him singing earnestly just before dawn—one last song! His gratification that the ceremony was completed when it was finally done! The decades it took for Dusty to enter a tipi again!

Hunter and Austin pulled him up from the ground this morning. Then he refreshed himself, making certain all the morning duties were completed before returning to the tipi. Laying his cane down near where he sat last night, he was able to lay back on the ground briefly to stretch his spine since the tipi was no longer full. He didn't plan to sleep until evening, out of decades of discipline.

He listened to people laugh and visit. Most were Cody's relatives or his. Some were old timers like them who hardly recognized his children anymore, with the exception of Hunter and Austin. Their acquaintance with Cody or him brought them here.

In the tipi, one young man was speaking, "Last night I thought about how this ceremony came over here and all the old people who first used it..." The conversation seemed far away from him, as if he listened and watched from a hilltop to people talking and moving about below.

"Little Man, Wind, Little Singer...," replied Cody.

"Is it true that a white man also helped with it?"

Cody nodded.

"Who was it?"

"His name I've forgotten. He was different from others of his time."

A rare man... In any generation...

Chee first heard of him when he was ill and his very life was at risk, the only time ever when illness overwhelmed him and his condition created more work for Susie.

The young man pushed for more information, "How did he help?"

"It's told that when this ceremony was receiving harsh criticism far away from white people who didn't know anything about it, he travelled to the Indians, talking with those who used it. He came into the ceremonies. Then he went back to his people and told them that the ceremony wasn't what they thought. But his opinion had no effect. Finally, he came back to the Indians and told them to organize themselves, then others had to leave this alone."

He understood his people… He knew what was at stake…

As he listened, grandson Eric passed by. He put out a hand so Eric could help him up. While his body had rested, his mind had leaped forward to other matters. Already he had a plan for the day, and when Eric stood him up and returned his cane to him, he went to seek out Susie to learn what she had to say. Yes, he could do things his own way if he had to, but part of his life's challenge was to include her.

He entered a busy and noisy house. Visitors were everywhere. Austin held a laughing toddler on his knee. Mabel and Dusty were nowhere in sight and neither were their daughters. Susie sat on the couch watching all the activity and helping half a dozen cooks find various cooking utensils.

He came in slowly and sat down beside her. Both quietly watched their children come and go. "What do you say?" he finally asked.

"It's good," she replied, taking her time with him. "It's good we did this. Now it's done. The meal will be ready soon. Then everyone can go home."

"Where's Dusty?"

"With his family…" She pointed.

"I thought about granddaughter all night. Dusty's daughter. What's her name?"

"Harmony," Susie answered. She couldn't pronounce the r sound. He repeated what she said, missing r and all.

"Dusty says she's very ill."

Susie nodded, "That's what he says."

"We have many ways to help."

"Yes," Susie agreed.

"Shall we do it?"

"Way back that's what you said."

That understood, he pulled himself up and went outside.

By then Cody was sitting alone there and Chee joined him. Neither spoke as they observed everything. Around them children raced, lazy dogs settled under junipers, and noisy jays landed in treetops. The two old-timers rested in all of this.

After the meal the young people planned to take down the tipi and help put everything away in the house and outside. Then everyone but he and Susie would depart. Take up separate lives again.

Very deliberately he took a long deep breath, held it consciously in his chest for a few seconds and then witnessed it going out. It was the same force the birds rode and caused flames to burst. He hailed it. No, he never accomplished anything alone.

Vows... Holy wind... Sacred ground...

Susie

SHE WAS A fierce protector. At necessary times she had been a mountain lion. That's the way she remembered it. Not just for Dusty. There were strings of grandchildren and great grandchildren. Her habits had changed only as much as her physical body was unable to carry out what her heart wanted. That bloom of earlier days was gone. Her will was still intact.

It's always there...

She thought of each offspring who came home in the last two days and those not there. She held no grudges. Distance occurred naturally and life had to be lived where it was.

Now it's done... Once more...

She came out of the tipi that morning clinging to granddaughter's forearm and she stood in the sun, staunch and venerated. Her family embraced her and she returned hug for hug. Then the homestead in her care called. Livestock in the corrals wanted attention. Food had to be prepared. She had to get going.

That's life... Motion... Movement...

Mary

SHE WASN'T PREPARED to meet so many people that morning at her mother's house because she didn't know of the plan for a ceremony that very night. She saw the white tipi in the distance.

Stop...

She considered turning the car around immediately, but it had been nearly a year that they had come this far to visit. Actually, it was Lester's suggestion. She kept her foot on the brake for a couple of minutes, then hesitantly steered toward the house.

Embracing the whole family, it was her brother Austin she held for the longest time, recalling the morning he was born, nearly fifty years earlier. Then she and Lester went into the next room to wait for a place at the table.

She focused on the tipi outside the window. Lester seemed to be curious about it; he'd never been this close. He went outside and very quickly was beside it, looking up at the eagle feather blowing in the breeze. He walked round and round the tipi with his hands in his pockets. Then he went back inside, his hair tussled around his face.

"Eat," she said to Lester as she visited with Keith.

Keith laughed and asked Lester. "Are you going to help butcher the sheep?"

"Truth is I forgot how," Lester answered with a friend-ly broad grin.

How different Lester is away from our house...

"Naw, you don't forget that!"

Finally, her father interrupted them, "See?" indicating the tipi. "We're doing something here for your brother, Dusty, tonight." He slowly stirred a cup of tea. The spoon tinkled against the cup.

Mary's silence was rare. Even Lester turned and eyed her, a move which she found quickly annoying.

Later she asked, "What's wrong with my brother?" Her concern was real.

"He's not himself anymore, hasn't been for a long time," her mother admitted.

"He should be in a hospital," Mary suggested.

"He's been there. Many times."

"They can help. With modern medicine, doctors..."

Lester began to cough. He wandered into the next room, then outside.

After they both helped butcher a sheep, they climbed back into the car.

"Coral's coming over here tonight." Lester said as Mary started the car. "That's what she said. She wants to be here."

More softly, he said, "Her husband's going to war—Vietnam."

You knew... You didn't tell...

11

The next morning, sun splashed the room. Mary sat rigid on the edge of a white dinette chair. Her whole body yelled no and her jaw jutted out. Earlier Lester came in quietly, fully dressed, washed and combed, and there was a woodsy scent of shaving foam surrounding him. He circled the kitchen a couple of times before taking a chair, drumming his fingers on the table. Then the tapping stopped. She turned to him, startled by piercing clear green eyes she hadn't seen in years. He lifted his chin and suggested softly, "Let's go over to your family this morning and spend some time with them. Let's do it for Coral and her husband." His words rushed out in a gentle trickle.

"It's Sunday, Lester!"

He put an elbow on the table, rested his shaved face in one hand and his eyes never left hers. He looked prepared to sit forever.

She shuddered. "That's not what we do on Sundays."

He ignored the protest. "Come on, Mary. Let's go."

Today he was strong and Mary shuddered again.

"It's time, don't you agree?"

My heart is stone...

She sat in a ray of light, unmovable, heavier than a boulder.

"I can't Lester!"

His eyes finally turned away. His fingers drummed the table again.

"Well then, Mary, I'm going to go over there by myself."

Her jaw dropped. "You wouldn't! That's not you!"

"Not for a long time," he answered calmly. "Today it is."

"But why?" she asked.

"Because I'm tired, Mary. Because it's time. Because Coral is over there. Because she needs us." He stood and nodded his head. Then he went out the door. She heard his footsteps outside.

Flooded with anger, her body shook.

"Lester! You... You..." Then she stopped her squealing and became very still.

This is the day I feared... The day I always knew would come...

Austin

$\int$ UNRISE.

He and Eric lifted the tipi canvas and placed it in the bed of the pickup truck. Its weight caused both of them to tug. Bulky, rolled into a heavy coil, it made a slight thump against metal. At his father's house, Keith, Hunter, and Cody planned to meet them and help set it up.

The two arrived before others. Austin filled the time with facts about the tipi.

"An old man made it for us. I called him uncle. He said, 'Use a clean white tipi for this ceremony. It has to be pure. Use it only that way!' We follow his advice."

Gone now... That old man...

"Sometimes I think this tipi is a book. It's been used so many times.

"The first time, your mother was expecting.

"It's helped a lot of people since then.

"One time, an elder was dying. Everyone gave up on him. He was an old timer who didn't want white medicine.

"His children caught and wrestled him down, put him in the back of their old truck and took him to a hospital anyway. He had a bed there, but didn't want to stay in it, and tried to sleep on the floor. He stayed a couple of weeks, but didn't recover. Doctor told him, 'It's hopeless.'

"He decided to go home. He walked out wearing a nightgown and no shoes. Some people picked him up and brought him back. After his escape he came here.

"He asked to use this tipi to make himself well.

"Your mom and I went to that ceremony. That night he really suffered getting rid of his illness. Next morning he was grateful. He lived a long time afterward."

Hunter drove up and waved, then went into the house.

"One time another man came over and asked to borrow the tipi ,too. He came with a young woman and they told us they planned to have a ceremony before they married. Your mother lent them the tipi but regretted what she did. She said, 'I don't feel good about it.' Turned out that young woman was too closely related to him, and she'd been going along with his plan for marriage because he took advantage of her since she was a child."

The tipi helped free her...

"Then there was the time an elderly couple had a grandson accused of doing something very cruel and bad, but they hid him, protected him as grandparents often do, even when our children are wrong. In the tipi he finally admitted everything was true; he was guilty of all that was claimed. His grandparents had no choice but to believe it then. It was hard for them to take. But, at last, they had truth.

"Another time, your mother's brother used this tipi. He's tried everything to stop drinking, including expensive doctors and counselors. 'Headshrinkers' white people call them.

"Nothing helped but this tipi and medicine. He's been sober now for fifteen years. His life is changed. 'It's a second life,' he says.

"The stories go on and on. This tipi is that kind of book."

Power...

Keith drove up. Three grandchildren were with him, two boys and a little girl who just climbed out of bed. Their hair was wild, bushy, and they had sleepy eyes. All went into the house.

Morning was brightening; little winds stirred.

A rack of tipi poles sat a few feet from the tipi ground, a smooth circle in a clearing surrounded by sagebrush. He and Eric marked the center of the circle; by then Hunter and Keith were lifting tipi poles from the rack, laying them on the ground. They selected four poles and tied them at the top with a long rope. Eric went inside the house to get his grandparents.

Cody arrived just then and waited for the old folks to come out.

His father came first; then his mother. She wore a sweater and the breeze swirled her long skirt, revealing another layer underneath. Behind them was Dusty, but he stayed back. He took a chair near the house, watching from there. Both his mother and father stood over the poles while Hunter said a long prayer. Then the elders went back inside. Austin, Keith and Eric lifted the poles into the sky using a rope to stand them up, placed them just so. One by one each remaining pole went up.

For my brother... For my brother...

Next Eric tied an eagle feather to the top of one pole and hooked the top of the tipi canvas just below that. They lifted it. After placing and securing that pole, Keith and Hunter pulled the tipi skirt toward the front, toward the sun. It fluttered out and fell into place over the poles.

Using a ladder, Eric laced the two sides of the tipi together with wooden pegs. All the red sides of the pegs faced the north and the blue toward the south. Then the tipi was staked down. When all was done two ear poles were lifted and slipped into the flaps. The tipi was taut and solid. The eagle feather flicked above the tipi and Hunter fastened the door.

Over the eagle feather thin clouds crossed blue space.

A car approached. Lily got out, carrying sacks of food and utensils.

Soon, the children in the house came running, "Eat. Eat." Everyone went inside except Austin. As he put his tools away Lily came toward him, dressed in old work clothes. She walked slowly to the tipi with folded arms. He leaned back on the truck and watched.

She circled the tipi, then lifted the door to look inside. She closed the door, tied it down, and looked upward. The eagle feather swayed directly above.

"Beautiful," she said.

↑↑↑

He divided his time between two homesteads that day, his mother's and the one he and Lily shared. All day while working, his children crossed his mind. They were thin clouds moving in the sky, particularly Eric and Melanie. He wondered if it had been a good idea to permit Melanie to come to the house tonight. Then he envisioned all the children of his brothers and sisters, babies to adults.

Unions... Departures... Reunions...

His day was spent in that awareness. When he looked at the ground, he saw the footsteps of all the children. Looking at the horizon, he heard their echoes and calls. There were many to consider. So when Hunter said, "Brother, tonight you'll be the one to talk to Dusty's children," he agreed. "They've missed a lot. You can teach them. You're good at that. You'll help like that."

As he planned for it, he understood that he would be speaking to all the offspring, no matter where they were and to which brother they belonged.

Uncle... Father... Son... Mediator...

When day became night and the tipi was crowded, it went the way Hunter wanted, easily, naturally. The younger ones in there expected it, slowly opening themselves to him and his words, words said thousands of times before but were new to them, coming from him.

Settling down after they entered the tipi, Cody nodded, allowing Austin to speak. He said in English, "My father and brother have asked me to explain this ceremony as we go along, for any newcomers. I'll just go over a couple of things for now."

Smoke... Communication... Prayer ..

Shortly after, he told how ritual items would move person to person, and how songs would go. He explained that water was brought in at midnight and at early dawn, keeping his explanations short. Through the night, he briefly explained selected details. At the close of the ceremony, he repeated some comments Cody made through the night.

For the next generation...

iv

When they came out of the tipi, he was in good spirit, going about visiting and helping everyone.

About mid-morning Melanie approached. She wanted to talk. She wore sunglasses over a serious face. He hoped to wait, give her his full attention later in the day when everyone went home, but she was set. Maybe she felt uncomfortable not knowing anyone here except him and Lily. After a time he gave in, pointing to a couple of seats at an empty table

She took the chair he indicated, removing the sunglasses, placing them on her lap. She began her story. She went straight to it, like an arrow.

"I was born a year and a half after my mother left here."

What?

He watched her youthful face, so much like Ramona's. He leaned his head to one side and a small sigh escaped.

"I knew about you from a picture my mother kept."

He knew the one, a gift from him. It was already worn and creased when he handed it over.

"I never met my father. He left my mother in LA. She had real feelings for him, but he was from Mexico and wanted to go back there. My mother never told him I was on the way."

What?

She looked at him and her eyes were red, puffy. She was embarrassed; he was shocked.

"I'm sorry," she said in a whisper, "You're probably really angry at me." He didn't respond for a while, just sat absorbing her presence, her words.

"You came a long way to find me. Why?" His voice was quiet, calm, searching.

"I don't know. I missed a family and thought I might find one here. But after I met you and everyone else, I knew what I'd done couldn't ever turn out right.

"Last night I sat out here, listening to the singing and other things that were happening in there." She looked toward the tipi. "I decided to take back what I said. You're not my father."

What?

She continued, "I'm ashamed of what I've done."

He sat silent for a long time, staring out at the crowd, and up at the sky. She made no effort to move either. She was weighty, iron.

"I'll tell her, too, this morning when I build up enough courage," Melanie said, turning toward Lily who watched all the children fly back and forth like flocks of birds.

Again he didn't answer.

"Austin! Austin," someone finally called. He stood and started to walk away.

"Aren't you going to say something?" Melanie asked.

He sighed again, shook his head no.

Dusty

TODAY HE STAYED outside from early light to late afternoon however strong the wind became. He was wooden. Sitting off to the side of the house, he didn't welcome company. Invisibility was what he wanted, turning his gaunt rigid self from the stream of relatives, making his expression impenetrable, and shrugging off attention by anyone who pulled up a chair

Hiding out...

In this period of life, each day was unsettled and today wasn't any different. It may have been worse. Judgment about everything he'd done filled his head. Events. Choices he'd made. He swung back and forth in time.

Then he went into himself.

It's my way... To be alone...

What was before him right then, curled protectively into himself in his hard, uncomfortable chair, was why in the world he agreed to this.

Second thoughts.... Second thoughts...

"I don't need it. I shouldn't have gone along with it." No one heard his whine uttered into wind.

Some people probably want to see this... Me weak... Suffering...

Yes, he knew he was unstable, had been for so many years. That certainty failed to show anything else to him.

Today he was facing himself and others, whether he wanted to or not. Expressions of his family showed concern.

"I don't want pity," he muttered after each person greeted him and then left.

He saw Cody arrive first in early light when the weather was still calm. The old man came to help put up the tipi. He watched Cody from the distance, finding his appearance the same as in earlier days, when Dusty turned away from his firm words and tone.

"Follow teachings of earth and sky... Follow elders..."

If there was any difference between then and now, Cody looked stronger, more wizened. That old man strode around in perfect physical shape, in contrast to him.

Stinging red pain always radiated in his chest, in a spider web. Sometimes it shot up his throat, made it painful to swallow or speak. His stomach often churned and his back ached all the time. He couldn't count on his stringy legs, either.

He rubbed his eyes, felt tears drip. Odd he felt them on his fingertips first, then on his face. He tried to laugh at his numbed body, tasting a salty tear. He hadn't really laughed in a while, and his face wouldn't move or break into the slightest hint of a smile.

Funny... No feeling... All my life that's what I wanted.... No feeling...

When Cody drove away, with a polite wave to Dusty, visitors lined up. He braced himself. Most came up close to look him in the eye, people he hadn't seen in ages.

Mary was a shocker! She'd come about mid-morning. They'd lost touch. She didn't have much to say, just held his hand briefly. Her body was stout, her eyes piercing. Her man stood behind, looking him over as if he was an insect, or something unknown, he suspected. The two stayed for an hour or so before leaving.

Hunter arrived, flanked by grandchildren; smaller ones darted in different directions as soon as Hunter started talking, "This is good, brother. To be family again." After sharing a few stories of old and new times, he slapped two leather gloves together and went toward the corral where he had plenty of work to occupy him until noon.

Richard arrived next with a beautiful young woman. His daughter! Happily, he hugged Dusty tightly. His daughter watched curiously and gave a stirring little talk to Dusty about her father's feelings for him.

It's too much...

Most visitors stayed briefly; then the homestead resumed its quiet pattern.

Slapping wind awakened him about noon to a larger presence than his own. Midday, it really let loose, threatening to topple him, or to pull him up and spin him in spirals like twirling pieces of green plastic turning loudly above. He leaned into those gusts, shut his eyes and mouth in a grimace, tightly grasped his chair, and refused to budge. That's how stubborn and reclusive he was.

As wind really kicked up, Mabel appeared at the door to join him for a minute. "How are you doing, honey? Do you want me to move the chair for you? You've been in the same place all day long." Her short hair blew around her face and her blouse and skirt ballooned out.

She carried one of his old shirts. "Do you want this? Are you warm enough?"

He was annoyed by her devotion to him, muttering to himself.

She leaned over to hear.

"I don't want your pity," He said through clenched teeth. That's what he wanted to say all day. His face was red with fury.

Mabel was stunned. She turned and went back into the house, but not before he saw her face. He didn't care how vicious his words were. He had no heart.

I'd run away if I could...

Later when he was hungry, he tried to stand alone and go inside. His chair blew backward in strong wind. A metal leg tripped him and he sprawled on the ground. Before he knew it, Mabel was there again. She was like that, appearing at his side when he was down.

"Come on," she said offering her hand. He ignored it. He turned over, in a baby's crawling position, and pushed himself up like a child just learning to stand. He walked unsteadily past her into the house, past his mother, and his daughters.

After he ate, he anxiously went back outside where he was most at ease. Alone again, he retraced events leading up to this day. Talks with his mother and father months ago. Disagreements with Mabel. His growing feelings of despair and hostility. Hunter and Austin intervening in his life.

The blustery wind began to settle. He was getting through another day and surviving his torments once again.

Not escaping fate, just putting it off...

↕

Something happened in the house. People ran in, rushed out. For the first time everyone overlooked him. Watching for a few minutes, curiosity got the better of him. Slowly, he made his way over.

Everyone surrounded the door of one small room. His relatives cleared a path for him as he took one labored step at a time. Odd, the way they let him by.

On a narrow bed was Harmony. Woody sat on a chair beside her, pressing a towel on her forehead.

What's this? What's this?

He made his way toward Harmony. Mabel stood at the foot of the bed, Faith and Rena beside her.

The room was quiet.

"What's wrong?" he asked.

No one answered.

"What's wrong?" his voice rose harshly.

Still no one answered.

He approached the bed and sat beside Harmony, squeaky springs giving way under him.

For the first time in a long while, he really looked at his daughter. Her eyes were closed, sunken in their sockets with shadowy green half circles under them from the bridge of her nose to the outer lashes.

She had diminished overnight. Her arms were skinny, sticking out of her blouse. Awkwardly he pulled the blouse around her waist and twisted it around her shrinking form.

Big changes... When?

Every day he saw and spoke to her. Something important had gone unnoticed.

"She's skin and bones..." His voice was hoarse, speaking more to himself than others.

Am I the last to know?

He yelled, "Mabel! Mabel!" though she was just an arm's reach away.

"Mabel, our baby's sick. Did you know?" He was panicky. He pulled the loose fabric tighter around Harmony's bony frame and looked up at Mabel.

"What's wrong?" he turned to Harmony again, taking hold of her hand.

Everything's a blur...

Woody sat leaning forward, his elbows resting on his knees.

That was the last thing he saw.

Then a damp cloth pressed his face and he heard Mabel tell him, "Everything's all right."

He was lying on the floor.

Woody and Mabel pulled him up and sat him in a chair next to the bed.

111

What he understood afterward was that Harmony, the daughter who was always teasing and laughing, the one who discovered humor in everything, was very ill. Her life was threatened. Everything Woody and Mabel said confirmed what he felt in his gut when he went into that room and saw Harmony's small figure laying there. Still, he was shocked, angered by what he was told.

"Who said that? Maybe it's wrong." His face was animated. His arms flailed out. He wanted to fight.

In a little while, the small room cleared. He stayed with Woody and Harmony, trying to take in the terrifying news.

Everything slowed. He stared at walls, heard a clock tick somewhere, but time stopped. Nothing was important, not even the reason he was here at this time. There was only dark uncertainty and doubt. More of it. More.

My daughter's life is threatened... Such a young woman!

Mabel placed a chair beside him. His father sat down.

"It's not fair!" Dusty choked.

His father held his cane in front of him, crossing his wrinkled hands over the handle after he sat down. He tapped the floor with the rubber tip of the cane and waited.

Dusty faced him, reaching for Harmony's hand.

"Harmony's really ill. Maybe she won't get well." He was sobbing. "I didn't even know! I didn't even know! I see her every day. I should've known!"

His father let him carry on like that for a while. When he became more emotional and hysterical, his father finally held up a hand, putting a stop to it.

Only then was he able to see his father's winters and frailty; only in that pause, and only without the hysteria. His father was dressed in a gray sweatshirt, and jeans, the legs folded at the bottom into cuffs so that he wouldn't fall over the long pant legs. His work shoes looked too heavy for him to lift.

Still, he had streaks of blue-black hair mixed into the cushion of light gray and his brows were very black. His father was serious; the skin on his forehead pushed up into a thin frown as he listened, while Dusty looked back and forth at him and his daughter. Back and forth. He was close to something in that observation, but pure emotion surfaced again and whatever it was that was near, moved away again.

"It's not fair. Why try to overcome all this?"

I'm afraid...

From his father, his eyes went to Mabel. He felt tiny and unworthy of both of them.

His father replied, "As long as we draw breath, there's possibility."

That's what he would say... That's what he would say...

That response made him pause. Next, he became fury itself. His eyes lit in a fiery flash. His heart beat speeded up and a roar filled his ears. Then just as quickly, fleeting seconds later, amazingly, he felt a wee bit heartened by his father's comment and all the tightness in his body went out from it.

He let go a deep breath, deciding to voice other fears then, those thoughts which circled in his mind much of the day and made him crazy. He tapped his skinny thighs with nervous fingers as he spoke. Anger carried him away.

By then the room was empty and they were alone except for Woody, still watching over Harmony.

"My father, I'm not the man you are," he nearly screamed. Woody looked at him hard. He brought his voice down. "I've never used these ceremonies since I left here for good. I didn't think they'd help against the world out there."

He closed his eyes, willing his tears and anguish to stop long enough to organize his words. His face flushed but he was able to lower his voice even more.

"You live by medicine and all the other ceremonials. All your life, that's the kind of man you've been. I wish I was like you, but I'm not."

Brash though Dusty's tone was, his father didn't turn away at all.

What did I expect?

His father nodded. "Right now, it appears that everything's too hard, not worth struggle and pain. But it's still possible to overcome that harmful thinking. It's still possible to do something for yourself. To help your daughter. To help your family. Even in your condition, there's possibility."

Suddenly, Harmony's hand pulled away, and he looked at her. She was alert, staring at him with recognition. He leaned over and hugged her, remembering her face when they first met, a face of a child. Almond eyes.

She squeezed his fingers and turned on the bed to rise again.

"I'm all right, Daddy," she said. "This has happened once or twice. What about you? Are you all right?"

She was calm, matter-of-fact.

Woody stood, walked around to the other side of the narrow bed to help her stand. When she and Woody left the room, Dusty turned his attention once more to his father.

"I agreed to use this ceremony again and I will. Shall I tell why?"

His father didn't answer; their eyes locked.

Dusty looked in the direction Harmony and Woody went.

He may as well confess all. "There's no other place to go. Other men might go a different way. Another kind of church, maybe. Another religion. Some people told me to just go to other doctors. But this is me."

His father kept his eyes on him, listening with all of himself. It took Dusty by surprise but didn't make him change in anyway.

As long as he had gone this far, he had to add more, "My father, I may as well admit I don't know how to behave in the tipi any more either. I've been absent too long.

"You said way back that truthfulness should be there. I don't know what it is anymore." He felt broken, incomplete.

His father was still looking deeply at him, into his soul. Then his father nodded, his face unreadable. He pulled himself up, left the room, and Dusty sat there alone, chewing on things said and done.

Confession... Sad truths...

By then, the rest of the house was starting to fill. Eric brought in two young men. Hunter's wife and another grandchild appeared. Austin and Lily were with Melanie. As sun set, vehicles began to surround the tipi. A stream of visitors entered the house. There were elders and young people. Most were blood relatives; others were clan relatives, a couple of them were strangers.

When Cody arrived the second time, he finally accepted the fact that all the day's activity was for him.

It's very humbling...

Watching Mabel dress, he noted her strained face and swollen feet. An unexpected rush of tenderness filled him. He allowed himself to be moved by it.

When she set out clean clothes for him, he found enough courage to stand alone, go into the back room and change. Slowly and carefully he washed his face and combed his hair. He saw himself in the mirror and shied away from that puzzling image, a leaning, sickly figure and a face he no longer knew, a scarecrow.

Then as he watched his daughters prepare for the ceremony, a change of mood filled him. It was the closest thing to being hopeful in a long while. They combed their hair and put on clean dresses. His gaze kept returning to Harmony. What was going to happen to her?

Second thoughts...

"Harmony, stay in the house tonight. Rest here. You haven't gone to this before. It's hard sometimes. Weak like you are, it's better to stay in the house."

Harmony looked him in the eye, shook her head no. "I'm going with you. Woody will help me. I'll be okay. Rena and Faith will be there."

"But you're not well, baby," he countered.

She answered, "So are you. Besides, Mom said this is what ceremonies are for."

SHE reassures me... Life's different than we expect...

It starts from here... Breath...

He had calmed himself. He wasn't sure how. But after the talk with his father, he'd followed all the activity in the house only with his eyes and ears, and kept his mouth shut. Saw sky and earth outside seep into the house. Saw his father go outside and become part of streaming sky. Saw himself watch all those scenes pass by. Heard his mother's voice and others pin him down, so he didn't drift away from himself. He took another deep breath. Waited without waiting.

When his father beckoned, he squared his shoulders and followed, leaning on Mabel's arm. They crossed sandy ground and went into the tipi's glow. They were on the edge of darkness; day calmly merged into shadowy softness and comfort. No one knew how winds had beat on him earlier, rattling his bones and threatening to do away with him. Between the house and tipi stood Hunter and Austin, sentinels watching their father make his way toward them.

Inside the quiet tipi, he was even more comforted by the presence of his daughters taking their places on the other side of Mabel. Harmony settled down beside Woody already waiting there. Dusty leaned around Mabel and stared intensely at each daughter. They were flowers, stirring something tender and deep, forgotten inside him.

To his surprise, the tipi was nearly full; flame rhythmically shot up from crossed logs. The perfectly molded altar was ready, and the fragrance of sagebrush found him. Everything was in order and all of it was pure.

Eric sat on the right side of the doorway as he entered. He saw his niece, Coral and her husband, along with Hunter, and his mother. A couple of faces he didn't recognize.

After Cody took everyone outside and brought them in again, Dusty tried to remember the steps and order here.

When Hunter put incense on charcoal and the tipi filled with its sweetness, Cody stood, lifted a small flat button and purified it in sweet smoke. Then he placed it in the center of the altar, in the groove going from tip to tip.

Then Cody said, "We'll begin now." He turned toward Chee, "Do you wish to speak?"

His father called Cody "Uncle," though Cody was younger. He welcomed everyone to this place. Then he heard his father say, "My son here, Dusty, is who this is for. With him are his family, his wife, three daughters and an in-law. They all live in town. He's not well. His illness is in his mind and body."

His voice shook. "I want good lives for each offspring. That's why we're here. "

Afterward Cody asked Dusty to speak.

He didn't respond for several seconds. They stretched into an uncomfortable period of time. Cody was patient. Mabel shifted around uneasily. Others in the tipi went along with Cody; some looked directly at Dusty as time stretched out.

Finally, he answered. "Yes, thank you."

He'd been trying to put his thoughts in a row. He knew all day and all week that this moment would come.

It's painful to ask for help...

He was almost unable to admit he was here because he had a problem he couldn't answer. He didn't want to say he needed help. It was difficult to ask everyone, relatives and strangers, to meditate about his life and encourage him. He never did that before, or exposed himself this way. It didn't feel good. He wrestled with himself.

I can't do it...

He cleared his throat and said weakly in Navajo, "I'm Dusty..."

He mentioned his parents' and their clans, and both grandfathers and their clans. He looked at the ground in front of him and kept his eyes there.

"Beside me is Mabel. These are my children, Faith, Rena, and Harmony. Over there, that's son-in-law."

Here he switched to English. His eyes went to the altar. He spoke haltingly.

"Most of my life — I've been a loner. Now, something has caught me. It attacks all of me, too. I'm sick all over and all the time."

He became emotional.

"I've taken drinks now and then. That has a lot to do with it. All I know is I don't have what I need to live anymore. I'm missing something."

This craziness inside me... I still don't want to tell on it...

His voice broke. When he regained composure he went on, "I make too many mistakes. Wrong decisions. I hurt people. It's the kind of man I am."

I don't want to own up to all this...

He looked up from the ground, scanning the circle of faces as he tried to find the right words. His vision blurred from tears but in the blur was a woman sitting across from him, someone slightly familiar.

He leaned over and looked around Mabel at his daughters to steady himself.

"That's what's wrong, why I'm sitting here. But this woman by me and my children — they're what I've done right in life. I don't want to hurt them no more. Then there's my mother and father who care for me. Today, I see how old they are, how strong their feelings still are for me.

"I don't know what's wrong with me."

Everyone listened, and at the conclusion, a couple of them replied, "Yes, yes."

Next Mabel was asked to speak. She seemed uncertain and nudged Dusty.

"Go ahead," he said.

What will she say?

"Dusty always says he has no reason to live," she said awkwardly, her eyes still on him.

Dusty's daughters were given a chance to speak but each was quiet.

Everyone made prayer smokes and Austin said to Dusty's family, "Now, it's time to talk to the holy people. Sometimes we speak our prayers out loud, but you can say them to yourself if you want."

Cody started in a firm voice. Dusty's father joined and then his mother. All around the tipi, more voices joined. Men and women prayed in Navajo and English. Some mentioned Navajo holy people, some called upon God, some addressed Mother Earth, and some spoke to Grandpa Fire. Their whispered prayers were like soft distant thunder, rolling around the circle of the tipi, rolling around Dusty.

But nothing from me... I have no words...

He was self-conscious. He couldn't even imagine structuring a prayer. Who would he pray to? He'd forgotten the holy people, maybe he never knew them. "God" was even stranger, coming from his lips. At his side, Mabel whispered a soft prayer in English. Faith had her eyes closed; she sat motionless like a beautiful statue. Rena watched her mother; that she was a copy of Mabel, Dusty hadn't ever seen before. Harmony sat unblinkingly, staring at each person there in the crowded tipi. Woody said something about the Holy Spirit.

Still no words. Dusty was empty except for criticism.

I can't even think of smoke as a spirit no more... I'm too much on the outside now...

Next to Woody, his father prayed easily in a soothing tone. He heard part of what his father said. On the other side of his father, his mother mentioned Dusty's children and future grandchildren.

All around the tipi everyone was intent upon him. Some mentioned their own personal accomplishments and conflicts, but everyone talked about him and his family.

Afterward medicine went around the circle.

V

Dusty received a stem of fragrant sagebrush which came before the medicine and he looked at it.

How's this going to help me?

He took it and followed the procedure anyway, blessing himself with it but knew in his heart the emptiness of his act. Then the medicine came. He swallowed it before passing it on to Mabel.

All three daughters sat on their knees as they took the medicine.

Drumming started, the gourd rattle swished, and Cody began to sing the opening song. The familiarity of the ceremony started to come back to Dusty. Unconsciously, its return led him to look deeply at the home he started from and his life after. Thus his meditation effortlessly began, taking off on its own. Taking him to places he hadn't gone in years.

Soon the drum and staff came to him and he passed them on. Shortly afterward, Cody was praying again. Dusty observed him.

He sat with his legs crossed and a glint of metal encircled his wrists. Cody looked at the altar before him as he prayed. On the other side of the tipi, someone sang. The fire burned bright in the center of them; sparks made small popping sounds. So the first part went.

After the first hour, Dusty's back and whole body began to rebel at sitting in one position and the ceremony was barely starting.

Then his military years and that training and experience came to him. His military life had never stepped forward like that.

Sitting for hours, days, weeks....

His body responded favorably to those images and it remembered how to wait.

Sit. Sit. Wait. Sit.

After a while, he became drowsy and couldn't keep his eyelids from dropping. He felt Mabel's head drop against his shoulder a couple of times, too, though she tried to stop herself. She looked at him and smiled. "I didn't know how tired I am," she whispered. Dusty fought the same fatigue. Around the tipi, others were alert, singing and praying. He sat passively against a tipi pole before surrendering to quick little naps. Either Hunter or Mabel nudged him to sit up straight when the drum and staff passed, or when medicine went around the tipi.

About midnight, he saw a forgotten child his mother and father had.

THAT Dusty...

Opening his eyes wide, he gazed around the tipi; Harmony stared at him. Mabel had her eyes shut. He closed his again. Saw himself again about the age of three, with shoulder-length hair and a faded red shirt. He also wore short pants. He had no shoes. Still, he was happily chasing a chicken, waving his arms to frighten it, rushing madly toward it. The hen dashed away, round and round the juniper trees, making loud clucking sounds. Finally it turned and flew at him, a feathered ball. The memory was brief. Vivid.

Beside him, Hunter sang.

Touching songs...

Dusty felt emotional.

Then midnight water was brought in.

The interval afterward—from the brief break after midnight to bringing in morning water—Dusty expected to be a long stretch. However, it didn't go that way. He became fully alert once more, when for about an hour all the singers were in perfect unison, and the drumbeat and the flicker of fire joined together seamlessly. Everything was a single stream of light and sound.

Shadows at the apex of the tipi, cast by everyone's movements at its base made him look up. At one point, all the shadows converged up there and became an image of a bird, fluttering melodically.

All during that, people continued intense words for him. Those prayers were usually long and in Navajo.

Finally, it was Dusty's turn to do that for himself.

My turn...

That, too, was easier than expected. At first he couldn't open up but got past it, the block within him.

He began to speak. Just speak. A mountain he crossed.

Once he really got going, words came out of his mouth like living things, and some tears flowed. Yet he had so much more to move out of the way.

Clear my head... Push... Pull...

As the drum moved from singer to singer on the other side of the tipi, he recounted his life history. Humiliations. Achievements.

Cody occasionally said, "Yes, yes," in response to his words. Finally, Dusty wound down.

He had laid out the most critical things. He said a few words he always wanted to say to "God" if he ever ran across Him. He had asked a couple of the questions saved for Him over the years. Then he closed his prayer. "Another chance. I want to start over again. I can do better. Do the right thing now."

He paused.

Ah, but talk's easy... It's the easiest thing...

After that, the rest of night rushed on. When Eric went outside to get more firewood, a gust of cool early morning breeze filled the tipi and Dusty realized the ceremony was nearly finished.

Waiting for the ritual breakfast, his eyes went from person to person, until they came to the woman sitting across from him. They lingered there and then moved on to focus on the others in the order they sat. Then his eyes went back to the woman again. She was whispering to the man sitting next to her

Could it be? Could it be?

At the close, Cody asked him, "Do you have anything more to say?"

He nodded. He had survived the night, just as he had survived his life. He thought about it and a very faint smile slid over his face.

He said, "Last night I didn't know what was coming. I was all angry. But this morning it's different. I feel all peace."

He turned to one side and said, "My father, thank you. I guess I'm the lost sheep. The one we always had to go back for and find. I never liked that sheep because of all the trouble it made. Sometimes I threw rocks at it when I found it. You always tell how much you love your sheep, how you know each one by sight, how important they are to your life. I guess the teachings in herding sheep come into the tipi, too.

"And my mother, thank you. What you gave me, I will take better care of it."

He turned to Mabel and his daughters and thanked them, then on to everyone else in the tipi.

Facing Cody, he sighed deeply. "I'm ready to turn my life around."

He gulped at what he said. He gulped at who he said it to.

Just talk again?

Cody stared back, steely-eyed, eye to eye, but this time Dusty understood what he didn't before.

At a signal from Cody, the fire man opened the tipi door and cold air swooped in, bringing a clean fresh scent. Everyone rose in an orderly fashion, helping one another stand. Dusty was on his feet and went out the door supporting himself with a cane. The line of people ahead of him raised their hands to the east and greeted each other. He joined them. Finally, the crowd broke up; Dusty's daughters already ambled off and Mabel was gone too, after looking in his direction.

vi

Someone tapped his forearm, and suddenly there she was, right in front of him. She faced the sun and squinted at him. She gave him time to place her.

What? What?

He greeted her awkwardly.

"Do you remember me, brother?"

How does a man forget the blunders he makes in life?

"It's been many years," he admitted.

She had a little more weight now. Otherwise, she looked the same, still favored traditional clothing and hair style.

After all the years, he didn't know what to say.

"It's good to see you and talk to you again, sister."

Just then the man she was with came up and held out his hand.

Dusty took it and introduced himself.

"Yes," the man replied. "That's what she told me. She said she heard of this ceremony for a long lost brother, someone she hasn't seen since she was a girl. So we came. We're here."

"My husband," she laughed.

"Yes, I told him how we went to school together but I didn't fit, so I left."

Dusty was flustered by her openness. His past was coming face to face with him again.

Can't run away from it... It's always here...

"I'm sorry," he said, his voice down. "Sorry for what happened." He was sincere.

Her gaze shifted from all the people there. She looked directly at him and answered easily, "Well, that's gone; those young people are gone.

"You probably don't know, but I went back to school, another one that understood me better. It helped. Today, I'm a teacher! Our language, culture, are what I teach.

"I'm happy to see you and your family, and to hear that you want to stay in this beautiful place with them."

They parted. Dusty was surprised at her forgiveness, but even after thirty years, he flinched.

He stood there a while longer, deep in thoughts flowing from currents outside him, filling him. He felt full.

This morning his body and his mind were joined.

Parts of himself he'd cut away years ago were restored to him last night. They were tender and soft things, new sprouts in the ground.

And my heart...

He probed within himself, found it faintly strumming. He listened to it briefly, incredulous it was still there, deep down, working on its own time, following its own course.

VII

Waiting for the large meal to be served to family and community, he affectionately observed two of his daughters. The three of them were in the nearby *hogan*. Harmony rested on the cot. Faith sat alone, looking out the doorway. Rena was helping prepare the meal, along with Mabel. Woody was outside with all the men.

My heart feels full again...

Physically, Faith was a small-boned wisp of a woman, barely five feet carrying maybe ninety-six pounds. Daily, she walked hospital floors, then ran narrow side streets toward the evening sun "to clean out my head and open my heart" she told him whenever hospital shifts were too heavy, or when something blocked her.

Truthfully, lately he hadn't really listened to her or Harmony or Rena when they shared their lives with him.

Too caught up in me...

Now she turned unexpectedly to him. Her voice was all soft in the morning but what she had to say was hard.

"Daddy, you told us you've always been alone, but that's not true. You have this big, big family. Why do you lie about it?"

Her face was peaceful. Only her eyes gave her away. He strained to hear more.

"You should let go of some of your old secrets, too. You can't carry them alone anymore. Besides, secrets don't stay hidden. We probably know them all by now.

"Carmen? The child you two had? What else?"

She wouldn't look away, so he had to.

Early, as a teen, she was the one most likely to talk to him like this, always with this directness. Unexpected, without anger. She was the only one able to stand up to him and question his erratic behavior. She'd hold his hand and disagree with him or refuse a hasty explanation for his unkind words or acts. Face to face.

Now she pulled her chair closer but her eyes turned to the door again. Just then, some children they hadn't ever seen before stuck their faces inside; one was about four or five, with crazy stand-up hair. All gave blinding smiles and dashed off again; they were wild little things, loose on the world.

"There's something I haven't been able to say until today. Will you listen?"

He always did before. In the early years, he'd rest his chin on his knuckles as he tried to see what she had drawn out for him because something important had gone past him and he didn't see it until she showed him, with others who tried that, he was resentful and impatient.

"I don't know if Mom ever told you that she wasn't lucky with men?"

He shook his head, no.

"Well, she told us that once a long time ago."

Things happen...

She continued in a voice so soft and low that he wondered if he was hearing it at all, or making it all up.

Maybe I'm crazy again...

"Our family has had some hard times together, and at the same time, life's been really sweet to us, too."

He saw himself sitting now, listening closely. Then he melted away and only her voice was there.

"You're the only father I ever known."

Her words floated beyond him. That happened last night, too, with all the words said for him then.

"As fathers go, you're good at it."

Tenderness coursed through him. It hurt and it was joyful too.

She pointed out the door. "This morning light tells me we've had many days like this, beautiful ones, but we don't notice them enough. Today, Daddy, I know that some of this light, over the years, came from you."

Oh!

He tasted a salty tear on his lip.

The wild children stuck their heads in the door again. "Come here!" they shouted in Navajo.

"Okay," Dusty answered.

The one with wild hair stuck out his tongue at them and giggled hysterically. Then they all took off.

He and Faith looked at each other, couldn't help but roar with laughter. He wiped the tears from his eyes.

"That's all I have to say," Faith sighed.

From Harmony's cot, her voice followed. "I second that, Daddy. What Faith says."

"Well, let's go join everyone," Dusty said quickly, uneasy with his daughters' show of tenderness toward him. "What about you, Harmony? Want to stay here?"

She was beside him, throwing back her long hair over a shoulder, and reaching out to him.

"Now, take Faith's hand, too. We'll go with you wherever you want to go."

Teasing... She's always teasing... Isn't she?

Lily

I F NOT FOR *stories... If not for love...*

She unfolds a cold metal chair and plunks down near high flames outside, waiting to use an enamel wash basin balancing on a rickety table barely wide enough to hold it. A blend of sounds comes out of whipping flames: water splashing into the basin, the table creaking, family voices and motion, along with distant horses neighing in the corral, and birds perching and tweeting, high and low. She is witness to all of it, especially the fully illuminated ground looming larger than life, under almost cold airy light. From time to time in her life, the earth has risen up close like this, magnified. Not far away, Austin laughs heartily, turns, flashing a dazzling smile, caught in light in such a way that his presence and this day are joined, sealed.

Eric, nearly Austin's height, stands beside his father in the group of men over there. By the doorway of her house, Austin's mother leans into her old man as they make their way inside. A few feet away, tiny children waddle after older ones racing across the ground, some unwashed and still wearing night clothes, spirals of energy, spilling all their emotions, not holding anything back, screams, giggles, tears. To which parents each belongs she won't guess, their tiny faces soft blurs whizzing by, and copies of one another as they are. Close by, women in colorful aprons bring utensils to roaring fire and their combined voices are boisterous strains of music in the air.

Finally taking her turn, slapping her eyes and face repeatedly with cold water, she readies to greet clusters of relatives all around.

Lineages...

Early yesterday morning she arrived and has been here since. Events of the previous day and night are winding down and ending. For her, they started about thirty years ago and longer than that for some others here.

In her twenties and two years older than Austin, they first came face to face after an elaborate ritual held for him almost in this same location. Actually, because he was much taller, it wasn't face to face. Sporting a haircut of dark fuzz, he wore a military uniform with a striped tan and green blanket draping over one shoulder and a white headband across his forehead. That image showing the tender youthfulness in his face and lean body at that chance meeting sent her reeling earlier in the wee hours of today, this many years later.

She didn't know what youth really was then, even when she was part of it. She thought she knew. Her light brown eyes watered unexpectedly and she choked on emotion seeing his youthful self, up close again.

While Austin's image came on its own, it's more challenging to summon a fixed one of her back then. Nothing pops up. Remembered photographs don't help; hazy or clear, their projections of her are more distant over time. She doesn't connect to any. Each missed her. What she grasps of herself during all their years together is what she feels now, an eye-witness going through a sweep of seasons, days and nights. Observing Austin. Observing their children.

Observing their grandchildren. Witnessing seasons arrive and turn, flashing streaks of sight and sound, sharp, fading.

Shining streams...

When those seasons were closest and most full, she lost herself in their movement. Yet, here she is this morning, distinctly herself for this moment.

On the day the two met, no lightning struck, as she heard happened to other women; merely vague curiosity arose about a young man who already had returned from a foreign country and had the rest of his life ahead. She wasn't ever struck by that kind of love, as a girl or in midlife. She's still unable to imagine it.

Austin disappeared right after. His parents said, "California," when asked about him, looking past western mesas into sunsets and valleys and saying it wistfully with accents so heavy it prevented some from understanding. California, another distant land, she thought at the time.

Months later, they met again at a gathering for one of her grandmothers. Doing the ritual was an elderly man everyone affectionately called Mr. Baggy Pants, and Austin was his helper. By then his body had filled out and his hair, grown long, was pulled back from a very pleasant face. That time she noted an unhurried way of describing his ideas and plans and his light laughter as he told of them. How attainable his future sounded! His words—always a measure of a man—made her stop and study him, the way she often stared into a new day.

Life flows, turns...

With the exception of his war experience, and the ceremony which ended this morning, she and Austin had similar lives and stood on common ground.

Her mother and father, firmly traditional, nodded approvingly when she shyly said his name. "Good man," her father responded, turning from his work and squinting at her, seeing through the mist that she was. Other than that, whatever else her father thought wasn't told. He accepted Austin's life already and hers with Austin later. Her mother went along with it, patting Lily's hand or back, when Austin was present.

Forces drawing us together...

Before they married, Austin told her straight forward, "Lil, the rituals I do are what I am! Take me or leave me! Do what you will!" He gave a good-natured wink and waited.

She stayed.

Many seasons together should have made them solid. Up to now their days were full of work and each other's company. They spoke quietly to one another and considered the other's response. At night they looked into each other's eyes while reviewing each day.

Then Melanie arrived.

There was no warning. Not even the dogs barked or growled.

She had set up a sewing machine under the large picture window. As the sewing machine quietly whirred, a shiny new car came up silently. If she hadn't seen the hood glint, she wouldn't have noticed. The driver sat a few minutes before coming out. She was waif-like and light, with almost blond hair, perhaps as old as her own children.

Slowly she opened the front door.

A line of people always came to take Austin to their homes. They ranged from being school educated to the most traditional. Some were mixed blood. She expected one of them.

Melanie's gray eyes were intricately drawn with kohl liner, and her hair was loosely tied on top of her head. A hint of sweet fragrance surrounded her. This close, she realized her visitor was older than first thought. She saw it in those eyes, while the young woman's manners and uncertainty said otherwise.

"I'm looking for him." She handed a slip of paper over with Austin's name scratched across it in a beautiful even line.

"He isn't here right now. He'll be back in a couple of days."

Melanie stammered, "Uh, uh, are you his wife?"

"Wife"...

Melanie stammered again, "Uh, uh, it's nice to meet you."

An awkward pause. Then Lily took charge. "Why are you looking for him?"

She took a chance; some relatives teased and raised their eyebrows when she spoke that way.

Blushing at Lily's directness, the younger woman answered, "Uh, uh, my name is Melanie. I have the same last name as his." She let go a small breath. Luminous eyes swimming in black liner were wary.

"Well, Melanie, he's not here now. Come back later." She realized she sounded impatient. When Melanie didn't move, she added, "Do you wish him to do a ceremony?"

Melanie looked confused, shook her head, no, shifting her weight from one foot to the other awkwardly. Her dark blue shoes were meant for town.

Lily motioned her inside, out of a strong breeze and away from too-friendly dogs that appeared just then, panting and jumping. Melanie stepped forward, hesitantly.

Before Lily had a chance to say more, Melanie blurted, "He's my father!"

Surprise...

Lily slowly inhaled, her hand groping the doorknob as she closed the door. The younger woman waited. Neither spoke for a few seconds.

"Your father?"

Melanie nodded, biting her lower lip.

"Your father?" she asked again. Melanie just looked at her.

"Who's your mother?" Lily gulped when she was able to speak.

"Ramona..." She was going to say more but Lily broke in. "Where is she?"

"She died last month." Melanie sniffled, eyes glistening.

Lily masked the rush of confusion welling up inside her. It quickly became hot burning coals.

Life brings the unexpected...

"Don't I know everything about Austin?" she asked herself when Melanie left.

The rest of that day crept along while she wandered through their home, seeing their life together over and over. Her face kept changing, sullen, then pensive, then full of anger, then blank, then jealous, and back to anger again. Round and round.

The next day she visited Austin's mother and father who pulled themselves up slowly to greet her. Austin's mother insisted on sharing some canned peaches. Lily told them about Melanie.

"What?" the old man responded.

The old woman, too, paused, remembering Ramona. "She stayed here nearly a year. We didn't know she carried a child when she left. Many winters have passed since then."

Chee agreed. "Austin never mentioned her. Did she write to him?" He looked at Susie and shrugged.

"Austin must have known about Melanie! Surely, he

knew!" she snapped. The two old people halted, leaned back in their chairs, eyeing her quietly over their cups.

She caught herself, her face suddenly red.

"We'll find out when Austin returns." It was a voice of reason. Then Chee reminded, "You and Austin have a good life together. You have beautiful children. You have grandchildren!"

When she left, she was still shocked, still fuming inside.

The next day her emotions and thoughts continued to run wild. Towards noon, Eric returned from a three day trip to purchase a new truck. Hugging him tightly, she followed him like a puppy, close on his heels, without explanation.

Before riding off on horseback to look for cattle in the afternoon, he turned in his saddle, gazed down at her and asked, "Mother, are you all right?" He was all shadow surrounded by sparkling light. The horse was anxious, ready to go. It, too, was shadow, and he held the reins firm.

Pressing her lips tight, she nodded, motioning him on. *Mothers and sons...*

The horse trotted off, disappearing on the hill. She watched for a while, studying ground and sky, missing something.

Between Melanie's arrival and Austin's return from New York City, she weighed the past spent with him. Their marriage. The birth of each child. Other family events against this new one.

Observing Austin this morning, content with everything around him, she recalls the second time she confronted him, the dangerous time.

She sees herself, as in a dream, hurriedly dash toward him, make a small stand there in front of him and block his way.

"Why didn't you tell me?" She spoke tersely, quietly, when she really wanted to scream.

"I didn't know," he answered. "I didn't know."

They faced each other across what seemed to be a great drop, she looking directly up at him, full of fury — a barely contained storm. Unflinchingly, she gazed forcefully into his eyes. She wanted to strike out. Raw emotion was getting the best of her.

Austin took a slow breath, narrowed his eyes, watched her closely and pursed his lips. He calmly put one hand on his hip. His movement was fluid, graceful.

He waited; she pulled back.

Incredibly, that day was otherwise so full of peace. A string of pointy mountains was clearly visible sixty miles away and the sky was richly blue above Austin. He was exquisite, too, very alluring and strong, his skin coppery and hair and eyes silky black, with the sheen of ravens lifting and landing on the fence. A branch on the nearest juniper tree trembled slightly in warm wind beside them, its needles gently bouncing.

Transfixed, she looked far beyond Austin, beyond the mountains and blue sky, turned unexpectedly and went into the house, closing the door just so.

Today here he stands, his usual steady self, as if life doesn't change each day, each season. Now here she is, forever altered.

Yes, grudgingly, she is accepting Melanie's presence, her contradictory emotions settling. Nevertheless, this is a twist. Only in the last two days has she managed to make it less pressing than family attention on Dusty's ceremony. It's been hard to let go.

Something's been shaken… Turned upside down…

Then last night other forces intervened.

First, the tipi called. She went inside to restore herself after the long day and to consider her part in Dusty's ceremony, which she was to do early this morning. Instead, a story rooted in an earlier time and another place was re-lived, so vividly she forgot herself, became fully caught up in it and swept away. Only the flicking fire held strong.

With her at the time was her brother. He had made the fire and let her be.

Family...

Going into the tipi the second time, she sat down beside Austin with the circle of participants and she stopped struggling. She simply let things be, no matter how large, how troubling or threatening.

Everything else fell into place.

An image of the tipi canvas slipping smoothly down the poles without any hitch, when everything is right, came to her and she relaxed.

Fire burned soothingly, bright and high, in a soft whir, a few feet from the earthen altar, consecrated ground. Everyone waited to meditate on matters brought before them. A handful of them had done that their entire lives.

Persistence...

To sincerely complete her part in the early morning, her intent had to be as clear as the water she had agreed to bring into the tipi at dawn. For her there was no question she must follow through, see her behavior now for what it would bring. For a few seconds though, she wrestled with herself again. A part of her body and mind held back, didn't want to fully give in, to put aside the situation with Melanie. Was it pride? Willfulness?

Finally the other part of her won.

There's a stream... An unstoppable flow...

She looked at Dusty, inhaled slowly, and directed her mind. She stopped listening to what was happening outside of her. Internally, her heart tapped in the cave of her chest. Her breath and tapping heart were all there was.

She felt them work together and gave in to them. Soon her doubts, like great solid stones, cracked and broke up into tiny fragments. They blew away. What she saw in their place was space. Immense restful space.

Night went forth effortlessly, fulfilling itself as it always did since the first time, until the earliest signs of forthcoming light came. Time for morning water. Water Woman.

Lily gathered her things and went outside.

Dawn. Purity. On tiptoe, she lifted her arms, stretched, breathed in that holy world. Sky stayed black; east light wouldn't show for a bit. It was just a promise right then.

Deep, soft, living space... Bright whirling stars...

Gazing up at silvery and multicolored points arching up and over her, she talked to them. No distance existed between her and them. She pulled her red shawl tight around her shoulders. Silvery cold air filled her lungs and limbs. Renewal.

Behind her the tipi was glowing, a pulsating lamp. Crimson sparks sailed from the top opening, air-borne. A lot of hurried activity went on inside as the participants prepared for the closing part of the ceremony.

An eagle whistled. Four times it called. The drum began. A song began. Then the door flap lifted in a swish, releasing a spray of honeyed light, permitting her entry. Picking up the water bucket, she bent down through the entrance and carried it inside. Settling on the ground just inside the frame of the door, she uncovered the water, and immediately felt the height of lapping orange flames and crackling heat in front of her. Lifting a bundle of golden eagle feathers, holding them in mid-air between her face and the flames, she waited.

When the singing stopped, there was extended quiet. Then Hunter spoke. He was confident, speaking leisurely. "Dusty" he began. "Brother..."

She looked at Hunter, then Dusty. When her eyes landed on Austin, she saw him briefly as he was when they first met. That startled her. She saw seasons change and go, impersonal and eternal. Her eyes brimmed with tears.

Then she studied the alignment of the water bucket, the fire poker, the burning logs, and altar.

Stories... Everywhere...

She felt them in the eagle feathers in her hand. She looked at the white enamel water bucket, a white heron on the side facing her, and recalled how this water bucket came her way. Each symbol on it had something to say. She thought of the man who had put the colorful images there and his story, but she didn't know him at all.

All were part of her. Her thoughts. Her daily life.

Hunter finished talking to Dusty and others, and swung out his arm to cast sweet incense on glowing red charcoal, bright sparkling jewels. Incense wafted upward.

Now this...

Her thoughts spontaneously arranged themselves in shape of a prayer as the eagle feathers blessed the water. With ceremonial smoke lifting her words, she began. Sacred names first. Holy forces and natural things. Medicine, the herb a lost woman brought to her people a long time ago in a far-away place. That woman's revelation.

Then Lily introduced herself to all the sacred things around the fireplace before mentioning Water Woman and the woman's prayer always offered at this holiest time.

She moved on to Dusty, introducing him once more to holy forces always surrounding human effort. She reviewed his present situation and history, and explained what he sought this early morning. He sat unmoving.

Clear vision... Restraint...

She included Dusty's wife and children, and his mother and father, and brothers and sisters.

Ties...

She described all their livelihoods and generational struggles to keep ancient bonds with natural forces.

Laws of earth and sky...

On she went, to the history of this ceremony. Why they all gathered with Dusty now and why other tribes also gathered all over their sacred land tonight, having the same ceremony wherever they were.

Then she mentioned Cody along with each of his helpers and all the others present. Finally, she described her own weaknesses and challenges she had to accept and what she desired for herself, before talking of hardships all people shared: illness, separations, aging, and grief. Next, she spoke of reliance on old men and women, their experiences and ways, along with their loving and warning words, to continue being who they were in forthcoming days.

Beloved teachers...

Sometimes her words slowed because she paused to breathe deeply or to think deeply before going on. Her voice blended with sounds of burning wood and silent falling ash, and persistence of ceremonial fire. Occasionally, someone in the circle agreed with her. "Yes," they echoed or a man or woman nodded a head.

Consequently, her prayer was long, and she meant all of it.

Halfway through, a stream of calmness came to her.

Serenity...

It was suddenly visible in the tipi, in front of her and then inside her mind, sifting through her body. First it affected her sight. There was depth. Sharpness. Ceremonial fire so clear it emitted a steady pulse.

When she finished her prayer, the earlier rage and confusion were completely turned around.

Where does it go? What does it become?

In its place was wide open space. Infinite. Pure.

She poured a drink of water for Ground Woman, took a drink and blessed herself before passing the bucket of water along. It made its way around the circle while Cody spoke to Dusty firmly about the road of life.

Man's behavior... Natural laws... Self control...

Finally the water bucket returned, and she went outside to get the small ceremonial breakfast, completing her part in the ceremony. Hills and vegetation were becoming visible by then, solid. An aura shone in the east at the earth's edge.

II

By the time everyone went out of the tipi, daily life and patterns were picked up again. Sounds of people layered over those of plodding cattle, sleek horses, and sheep bunched together in the distance, and dogs and cats close by, and all those layered over earlier sounds of wildlife, starting at first light. This presence and its voices charged the day world, distinguishing it from what she always witnessed in dawn's wee hours. A concentrated hush before the splash.

Yet it's all one... Seamless...

Now she greets everyone again in a new day, its solitude broken by two crying children. Her eyes skim over them and go on to all the others gathered now to help finish all the work. Her gaze searches for the older men and women who sat up all night in the tipi and lingers on them. Something presents itself to her in each of them; she recognizes it and feels for it within herself.

Melanie appears, is coming toward her.

"Sister," her brother says casually at her side, "When we meditate like we did last night, we can overcome ourselves and our emotions. We expect it of each other."

Then he voices what she has been asking herself all along, as he sees Melanie. "Can you do it?"

"You sound like Austin," she answers.

He moves away, toward the tipi where the men sit.

She's able to answer that question this morning. Rage has burned itself out and she's free. Inside herself, she laughs a little bit. She feels raw, tender spots there, as she recalls the hardest things she has ever faced. They were like mountains, high and steep. Here, a small obstruction has knocked her down.

Everything she seeks is here, at her fingertips. Her eyes sweep endless land, the house, the tipi, the community and family. They call out to her. Home they say.

Sacred ground...

Melanie stands before her with teary eyes. "I have a confession," she says. Lily takes a deep breath and waits, but doesn't want to hear. She forces herself to open to what is forthcoming.

They face each other, look into each other's eyes for the first time, see each other for the first time. Anguish is on Melanie's face and in her bent posture, but there's contradiction as well. She's young, intense, fiery and impetuous.

Ah! I see...

Lily looks away because Melanie is uncomfortably near, again making her too aware of what struggle is and the way things are in this world. There's recognition of other things too.

Life's deep...

Light plays magically over land lifting and settling down again, rustling and rippling.

Melanie spills everything in a messy way. Rapidly. Incoherently. Abruptly she stops. "That's all. I'm sorry. I know I did wrong." She looks drained. She may collapse.

Lily doesn't hear what Melanie says. It all rushes out too fast, disconnected. It's like a short storm.

Lily doesn't know what to think or what to respond to.

Then her eyes settle on the tipi not too far away. It beckons once more. It sits serenely apart from a swift stream of too many thoughts and words, and it anchors her.

"Let's go over there," she tells Melanie. "It'll be empty. And you can take your time and tell me everything again."

The tipi *is* empty. Everyone has gathered around a table nearby, listening to someone speak over there. There were too many to fit into the tipi.

Inside is only space and restful silence, a great union between those two forces. She and Melanie step into it.

Sanctuary...

Author's Note

The stories of the woman who discovered the peyote plant on the present day border of the United States and Mexico vary considerably, due to factors such as stories being told in tribal languages, translations into English, and recording of these stories generations later. However there are some consistent elements which run through all of them. It is important to distinguish this fictional version, imagined by the author, from other recorded oral stories. For more study of them, the reader is encouraged to do his or her own research.

A New Perspective on Navajo Prehistory
BY HARRY WALTERS

EXCERPT FROM THE INTRODUCTION:

Navajo history is a story of a great migration of prehistoric people over the vast North American continent. This migration of Athapaskans began in the Artic northern hemisphere and ended in the Southwest as the Navajo and Apache people. Comparative studies in linguistics and physical anthropology have established links between the Navajos and Apaches with the people of the Arctic North, Northwest Canada and the U.S. Pacific Coast. Broader studies of these similarities also point to a possible connection with the people of Siberian East Asia in a not-too-far past.

... A large part of present Navajo culture is of Southwest origin and dates to the Southwest Acculturation Period. The present ceremonial system began to evolve when the ancestral Navajo settled into a social structure based on the matrilineal clan system. The acquisition of agriculture served to strengthen this new order, and when domesticated animals (sheep and horses) were acquired, Navajo life became an agricultural-pastoral society...

Examination of early Navajo stories preceding the ceremonials period (before the Fourth World) illustrates that the Navajo once lived in a hunter-gatherer patrilineal society. But with the adoption of agriculture, ceremonialism (as it is recognized today) began to emerge, and the people's lives evolved into a matrilineal society. This transition was finalized with the coming of ceremonial known as the "Blessing Way." Today, Blessing Way is the backbone of Navajo ceremonialism and society.

Harry Walters is semi-retired teacher of Navajo culture, tradition, and art, with a background in Anthropology. He is a respected Navajo Elder and consultant on traditional Navajo teachings and has co-authored papers in this field with other writers.